A Hint of Jasmine and Lavender

An Erotic Romance

a novella by

Allen R. Remaley

ISBN: 1-4140-5619-2 (e-book)
ISBN: 1-4140-5618-4 (Paperback)

Library of Congress Control Number: 2003099828

This book is printed on acid free paper.

Printed in the United States of America
Bloomington, IN

1stBooks - rev. 01/21/04

Dedication

For Brooks and Janine

Table of Contents

Chapter 1

The Encounter

Growing up in a Western Pennsylvania coal town in the 40's and 50's did not usually mean that a young man would become interested in foreign languages, university study and travel. Sure, small towns in that part of the country had those who spoke Italian, Polish and some German, but the boys in those little towns played football, they worked in the mines and they usually spent their life earning a living from low paying jobs and most of them spent too much time at the local bars on Saturday nights. Frank Sarvey could have been one of those boys. He played football, and like his father and grandfather, he did work for a short time in the mines. In spite of the fact that he excelled in school, he knew that he would never have the money to do university studies. Like most families in his small town along the Susquehanna, there was no money for college, and no one in Frank's family had ever completed more than a senior year in high school. After his parents divorced

2

when he was ten, Frank lived with his grandmother whom he loved. When she died shortly after he graduated from high school, there was nothing left for him in his little town along the Susquehanna. So, in order to escape the life around him and in order to see more of the world in which he lived, Frank joined the Marines.

Four years in the Marine Corps changes people. The Marines say, "The change is forever." For Frank, this was especially true. That four years he spent in the Corps was as good as any undergraduate school. He learned discipline. He learned how to take care of himself, do his own laundry and ironing. He learned manners, respect for others, that rank has privileges, that a man never enters a building or an eating establishment wearing a hat, that "Yes, sir." and "Yes, Ma'am." are accepted responses when in public, and that one never leaves a lavatory without flushing and washing one's hands. And, yes, Frank learned how to use automatic weapons, explosives and if necessary, how to take a life with his bare hands.

Since Frank's tour of duty in the Marines never gave him any trigger time—actual combat experience—a fact which left him thinking himself deficient; after all, a Marine was supposed to be in harm's way. Marines were called jarheads, leather necks and bullet catchers, expressions used to indicate warriors. Frank did not think of himself as a warrior, and that left him feeling somehow lacking. He was still confident, but he often wondered how a young man could spend four years in the Corps and never get a chance to earn a Purple Heart? When he thought about it, Frank found himself haunted by the fact of not having completed that for which he had trained. But, more than the fact of never seeing combat, Frank felt that he was lacking in other things, too.

Frank was an enlisted man, a sergeant, E-4. Because of his self discipline of making sure he was always squared away—not getting into trouble, always the best in passing inspections, and scoring high on advancement exams and interviews — Frank was placed in a position of special recognition, and he became an orderly to the Commander in Chief of the Pacific, a four-star, navy admiral who had his offices in Camp Smith, Hawaii, located on a hill overlooking Pearl Harbor. Marines were always those who gave special protection to navy admirals, and it became Frank's job to stay close to his boss, carry top secret messages and escort visiting dignitaries to the admiral's office.

Frank performed his duties with an excellence and work ethic learned in the Pennsylvania coal fields, on the playing field while in school, and at a place called, Parris Island, South Carolina, the training base for enlisted Marines. As an admiral's orderly, Frank worked with high ranking officers, and when given an assignment, he carried it out and performed above and beyond that expected of an eighteen year old Marine. Frank came in contact with foreign languages when escorting French officers through CINCPAC headquarters in Hawaii. The French officers were making their way back to France from a place called Vietnam and especially after the battle of Dien Bine Phu in 1954. The Americans had not yet officially entered Vietnam, and they were trying to learn as much from the French as they could before entering into that conflict. Frank could not converse with those he escorted into the admiral's office, and that inability to speak and understand French forced him to realize that this and other deficiencies had to be corrected. And, that was the moment that Frank realized that he should go to college and study at least one foreign language. In July of 1956, Frank Sarvey left the

Marine Corps, and with the admiral's help and the GI Bill, he matriculated at Penn State University in September of the same year.

Using the same work ethic he had learned in the coal fields and later perfected in the Corps (dig in spite of the fact that it hurts, always be on time, work to the bell, complete the task assigned), Frank excelled in college. Frank enrolled as a French major, earned high honors and spent a year abroad at the Universite Grenoble in France. Graduating cum laude, he was immediately offered a job teaching French in one of the public schools close to University Park where he had completed his undergraduate studies. After two years of public school teaching, Frank had saved enough money to spend the summer in France, and in 1962, he arrived in Paris where he would meet the person who was to make him think about what is said of Marines, "The change is forever."

Upon his arrival in Paris, Frank found a little one bedroom garret in the Latin Quarter very close to the Seine. Although larger and deeper, the Seine made him think about the Susquehanna, and he began to feel at home. From one window of his garret apartment, he could look down into the quarter and watch the groups of students and tourists from every country as they surveyed the sights and each other. The aroma of Greek and Moroccan cooking wafted up to him, and he soon became even more at home in this area where cooked carcasses of lamb and goat hung out in the open for all to see and smell, where seafood, breads and cheeses would lure hungry tourists into small, underground restaurants like the <u>Bon Couscous</u>, the place where he would meet Marie-France.

Having lunch at the <u>Bon Couscous</u> was something Frank had worked into his schedule on a once-a-week basis. He would always try to beat the lunch crowd by showing up at the restaurant at 11:45, and he would ask one of the French-Algerian waiters to seat him downstairs in the *oubliette,* a dungeon-like cellar where, he had been told, people in medieval times were left to rot. All this taken from the French verb, *oublier*, to forget, seemed to imply that those thrown into such a place were forgotten and left to die. Frank thought it ironic that this former dungeon were people were left to starve was converted into an eating place. Now, centuries later, the walls of this *caveau* had been white washed, tables with the perfect and predictable red and white checked tablecloths were appropriately spaced, and, on this day, no one other than Frank had yet arrived for lunch.

Frank took his usual seat at one of the small tables which was made for two people. He ordered a bottle of Algerian red wine and couscous royal, the specialty of the house. Frank knew that the French-Algerians who owned and ran the restaurant were proud of an Algerian produced product, and who knew how long he might be in Paris? Making friends in the Latin Quarter was not a bad idea, and Frank's tips at the end of his meals made him a favorite at Le Bon Couscous. As soon as the wine arrived, and while he waited for his couscous, Frank unfolded a copy of Le

<u>Monde</u> in front of him. The newspaper was the equivalent of the <u>New York Times</u>, and it usually gave the world news with what Frank liked to call, "a French twist." He found an article of interest concerning American tourists and began reading between sips of his wine as he waited for his lunch to arrive.

Moments later, Frank looked up to see a marvelous pair of legs descending the stairs leading down to the eating area. A young woman, seemingly alone, was being ushered in by the waiter, and with each step she took down the stairs, the woman's physical presence was revealed like a picture unfolding in an e-mail sent photo. Frank's gaze continued upward over her body as she descended the stairs, and every step she took was a reward for Frank's eyes. The young woman was stunning.

From her soft leather shoes, Frank's eyes went to her robin egg blue skirt, short for warm summer months, to a brilliant red, short sleeved sweater which covered what must have been a wonderful body. But, her face, as if the best had been kept for last, was radiant and beautiful. Her hair, jet black, provided the perfect background for such a beautiful face. Somewhat embarrassed that he had allowed himself to be so taken with the young woman's beauty, Frank dropped his eyes back to his paper but not before he acknowledged this newcomer with a slight nod of his head. The waiter seated the young woman directly opposite Frank at another table. She sat, facing Frank, ordered a white wine, and picked up a menu. From her conversation with the waiter, Frank guessed that she was Parisian; her accent left no trace of the *provincial* often heard in the quarter, and Frank once again found himself focused on this other diner.

Stolen glances at the young woman revealed a natural beauty. Her hair pulled back into a ponytail, dark piercing eyes, no visible makeup, and no presumptuous or pretentious style of dress gave this young woman that special singularity—that *Je ne sais quoi*—which set her apart from others Frank had seen recently. She did not look like a tourist. She carried no metro maps, special brochures and no camera. Her only accessory was her leather handbag which matched the color of her sweater. Her body was that which could have inspired photographers— slim, but yet full figured and skin which seemed as smooth as the leather of her handbag. Her clothes fit her snugly, and that emphasized the mystery of what they covered.

A Hint of Jasmine and Lavender
An Erotic Romance

It must have been Frank's gaze which first drew the young woman's attention. Sitting just opposite him at the other table, she acknowledged Frank's stare with a subtle nod of her head, and that gesture shocked him back into reality. Not ever thinking himself to be suave, Frank immediately and seriously apologized by saying, *"Mademoiselle, je vous demande pardon. C'est que je me suis perdu dans le moment. Ma faim et votre beaute m'ont fait perdre la politesse."* She smiled at his compliment and she asked if he was Parisian. That made Frank feel even more confident; getting a compliment on his French gave him the courage to continue the conversation, just small talk, but before long, both Frank and his new acquaintance realized that this chance meeting might lead to other get togethers.

Frank was, in his own right, not bad looking. His 5'11" frame was well developed, and his days on the football field and Marine Corps experience had brought him along from a skinny teenager to what some women would consider as a hunk. Clean shaven, short haired, something carried over from his military days, and dressed in dockers, button down shirt and loafers, Frank looked every bit the young college type out on the town. Perhaps it was the wine they shared. He had ordered a bottle for himself and had offered some to his conversation partner who accepted appreciatively. As they drank and talked together, Frank wondered why the warnings on bottles of alcohol did not read, "The consumption of alcohol often leads young men to make fools out of themselves." Before the young woman had finished her lunch, and after they had finished the bottle of wine, Frank screwed his courage to the limit and asked if she would join him for coffee at an outside café terrace and show him the city. The girl looked at him for a moment, seemed to realize that there was something pleasing and different about this American who spoke French so well, and she said, *"Pourquoi pas?"*

In their exchange of information early in their conversation, Frank had learned that the girl's name was Marie-France. How perfect could that be! A beautiful young French girl, an appropriate name for someone so pretty, and Frank had just started his summer vacation. Frank had some female friends back home, but none had ever made him swerve from his goal of getting an education and settling into a serious relationship. Maybe it was the setting—Paris, the Seine, summer in the

City of Light—but, Frank sensed that something was different.

Frank met Marie-France for the second time two days later in a little bistro in the Latin Quarter. There, Frank learned that his new acquaintance worked in the *Bibliotheque Nationale*, and that she had every Tuesday and Sunday free. In the weeks to come, the American teacher of French and his Parisian beauty went to the Louvre and gazed at the Delacroix, the Davids, the Gericaults, and then they walked across the Tuileries Gardens to the Jeu de Paume, the annex used to house the Impressionists before the Musee d'Orsay would be built to display the works of Renoir, Monet, Manet and other artists who fled the salons of the late 1800's. While they took in the colors and images painted years before, the two, newly acquainted, shared information about their lives. Marie-France, however, divulged much less of her past than Frank, and she was persistent in her wanting to know more about why this American former Marine had come to her country. She wanted to know what he did for a living, why he had chosen his vocation and how long he planned to spend in Paris.

The two young people spent the entire day together, and later that evening, they went to the artists' square, the Place du Tertre, in Montmartre, where Marie-France allowed herself to reach out and touch Frank from time to time on his arm, elbow and shoulder as if to test his flesh, his reaction to her and his feeling for her. Frank was very careful not to reach back. He admired this new friend, and he worried about being too affectionate in his response to her touch. He knew that she had not yet given him her silent permission to take the liberty of holding her hand or taking her arm in his.

Later, after taking a tea at an outdoor café, they took the metro to the *Trocadero and Le Palais de Chaillot* where, from the terrace above the fountains playing in front of the *Le Musee de l'Homme*, they looked out across the Seine to the Eiffel Tower, now bathed in the glow of a thousand floodlights. While Marie-France had seen the tower many times, this evening, with Frank, the famous landmark seemed to radiate a special significance, and she wanted to show her young American how magnificent the tower might be up close. On her recommendation, the young couple walked across the Iena bridge to the base of the tower and looked up at the massive structure weighing more than 7000 tons. Before they knew it, the two sight-seers were on one of the elevators leading to the first stage of the tower. On the elevator, they were pressed together by packs of other tourists speaking many different languages. Pressed in the little elevator cage, one upon the other, Frank could not help feel the outlines of Marie-France's body, and he reddened in the impossibility of not being able to keep his body from pressing against hers. She just laughed at his innocence, and she liked that. Thinking that he might never return to such a place and knowing that he had enough money to do so, Frank suggested that they have dinner at the Jules Verne restaurant overlooking the

Seine. This Eiffel Tower restaurant was expensive, but a table overlooking the Seine gave its diners a beautiful view of the city's magnificent landmarks, the Seine itself plied by its illuminated *bateaux mouches*, and onlookers who wondered who these romantic diners might be inside such an elegant restaurant. The *maitre d'* offered Frank a table with a window view, and once seated, Frank dug into some of the money he had saved for this summer's trip and ordered a bottle of Dom Perignon. When it arrived at the table, Marie-France's eyes lit up and she said, "This is such a good *cru.* Do you know anything about the makers of this champagne?" Frank admitted that he was familiar with the champagne, but he was ignorant about the company and its makers. Frank was happy he had ordered one of the best French champagnes; memories last longer if they are worthy of remembrance. Marie-France seemed to be having a wonderful time, and she and Frank finished the bottle of champagne, laughed, dined and talked until the restaurant was about to close. Before they finished their meal, Frank made another suggestion. He asked Marie-France to come with him to see his little garret overlooking the Seine in the Latin Quarter.

At first, Frank thought that he had overstepped his good luck. A beautiful French girl had agreed to dine with him on the Eiffel Tower, he had spent more than several hours talking to this wonderful and interesting young woman, and she had seemed pleased with the time they had spent together. And, now, without thinking, he had invited her to see his little apartment overlooking the Latin Quarter. He had done so with some innocence, and he was glad that he had trivialized his meaning by uttering the worn out phrase, "to see his etchings." It had even embarrassed Frank to suggest such a thing after such a perfect evening, but he did. Marie-France glanced at her watch. It was almost midnight. She looked into Frank's eyes and said, *"Ca sera bien interessant. Pourquoi pas?"* They took the last metro in the direction of St. Michel station, the favorite stop of most of the students who lived in the quarter where Frank had his little apartment.

On the train back to the Latin Quarter, Frank thought to himself. He had had the good or bad fortune to make the acquaintance of an older woman when he was a young Marine. Although he took part in no firefights in Vietnam, he did fly to Saigon on occasion as one of the orderlies to

CINCPAC. On one of these trips to Saigon, on his free time, he met a woman of French-Vietnamese descent, and although he never asked her age, Frank guessed that she was at least ten years older than he. What she managed to teach him, or rather forced him to learn, was all the things a woman wants a man to do to her during the act of love. Knowing that Frank would soon return to the United States or lose his life in one of the jungles surrounding the city, her teaching was not so much for Frank's benefit as it was for her. She wanted to receive sexual satisfaction from a younger lover whom she was sure to lose. She made sure that Frank learned quickly, that he practiced what he had learned, and that he retain what he had learned. His thoughts were interrupted when Marie-France said, "Ah, I used to study near here." They had reached their destination at St. Michel, the student area in Paris. The two late-night diners crossed a street leading up to Frank's building in the Latin Quarter, and they entered and started up a flight of stairs to Frank's garret apartment. Frank kept telling himself that there was nothing on his mind but that of proudly showing off his *pied-a-terre*, this little one bedroom sanctuary in such a bustling area of

Paris. And, then he smiled at his own naivete.

Once they had climbed the steps leading to his little room, Frank opened the door and gave a princely gesture with his arm inviting his French princess into the room. The evening was warm, and Marie-France was wearing only a light, silk blouse, skirt and summer sandals. She walked to the window overlooking the quarter and looked out on to the scene below. Frank moved closer to her from behind, and without putting his hands on her, kissed her lightly on her neck. Marie-France did not protest, and instead, she allowed her head to bend and touch his.

33

She then reached back behind her and pulled Frank closer. This time, Frank softly caressed her with his hands being careful not to touch the more sensitive and more intimate parts of her body.

Marie-France turned toward him, and she kissed Frank firmly and knowingly on the mouth, and while she did so, she removed her sandals. Frank stopped her. He simply held one finger up to his lips as if to say, "No, not yet." She seemed surprised. Then, he said, "Let me." He bent down, took one of her feet in his hands and slid the sandal off. He slowly traced her toes with his fingers and lingered there like a tourist in the Louvre who had gained the special privilege of being allowed to run his fingers over the smooth marble of the Venus de Milo. He did the same with her other foot. He rose, stepped back slightly, put his hands on her neck and traced its curves with his fingers tenderly turning her around with him at her back. He moved closer, kissed her again on the neck, and moved his hands to the buttons on the front of her blouse. As he undid each one, he kissed her tenderly behind her ears and on the back of her neck. Again, her head seemed to welcome more of the same. When he had reached the last button on her blouse, even before the blouse slipped from her shoulders and fell to the floor near her feet, he cupped her breasts in his hands, and he held them. Only her breathing accompanied the rustle of silk sliding to the floor. Moving his fingers to the snap on the front of her bra, he unfastened it and slid it off and let it add itself to Marie-France's garments waiting on the floor. She turned toward him and offered to Frank what had just been exposed. Frank accepted the offer, and he kissed each of her nipples, now erect, and his lips lingered on her only as long as would a butterfly on one flower bursting with nectar knowing full well that other such flowers awaited the flutter of its wings. Marie-France undid all the buttons on Frank's shirt, lifted it off him and added it to the growing pile of clothing on the floor.

There was no longer any reason to speak to each other. Words had been replaced with touch, questions were answered with a caress, a kiss, and the subtlety of knowing where to place one's hands and fingers was axiomatic. Frank slowly removed what was still covering Marie-France's body, and he led her to where he slept. There, he sat her on the edge of his bed, and he knelt in front of her. He kissed the smooth and hard surface of her belly, and taking one of her breasts in his hands, he traced the nipple with his tongue, swirling it around the now tense, erect and hardened part of this beautiful young woman. His tongue lingered at her nipple like a famished butterfly seeking the last bit of nourishment from a fully blossomed flower. The butterfly moved quickly back and forth across the abundance which was Marie-France's breasts, and once satiated, Frank lowered Marie-France back on the bed, and she exposed her wetness to him. He kissed her there and again used his tongue and lips to bring her to her first climax. He then lifted her to her feet, had her stand with her back to him next to a wall, and she braced herself with her hands above her head as she leaned against the flat wallpaper covered surface. Frank moved his body closer to hers and again cupped her breasts in his hands. He again kissed the softness of her shoulders as he explored her body with one hand, then the other. When she was once again fully aroused, he led her back to the bed, and repeated what he had done moments before. Just at the moment when she was about to begin her second climax, he leaned her back on the bed, lowered himself on to her, slowly penetrated her, and they came together in one long eruption of sound and passion. Hours later, on her way back to her own apartment, his ejaculate still wet on her thighs, Marie-France was aglow with pleasure and wonderment. "Who was this man, this American?" "How had she allowed herself to become his lover so quickly?" She told herself that she knew very little about him. She had so much she wanted to learn about him. Two weeks later, after lunches, dinners, walks along the Seine at night, and visits to museums and sidewalk cafes, Marie-France, prompted by what seemed to be Frank's sincerity, moved in with him at the garret apartment in the Latin Quarter.

Marie-France knew that she was attractive, and she had taken other lovers, not many, and none of them were ever considered serious. But, Frank, this American, this former *soldat de la marine,* was different from the rest. Frank had made sure that Marie-France was completely satisfied before he allowed himself to fully enjoy her body by venting his passion inside her. There were even times that Frank would only make love to her, bring her to climax, then simply hold her without satisfying himself. No other man had ever done that with her. And, the bliss both of them enjoyed lasted until they went to the *Marche aux puces,* the largest flea market in the world located at Clignancourt in the eighteenth arrondissement in Paris.

If you were to describe the *Marche aux puces* to someone who has never experienced it, you might say that it is the largest garage sale on the planet. Open only on Saturday and Sunday, thousands of people, Parisians, tourists from every country in the world, children who come to play and run among its stalls, pickpockets who specialize in lifting passports and foreign currency, and those who are looking for anything from a Louis XV writing table to an eighteenth century copper bathtub used by some member of the aristocracy in pre-revolutionary

France, all these people and more move in huge circles among the immense array of goods, junk and fine art and antiques. Frank had been there before by himself looking for old military paraphernalia. Once, he found a Zippo inscribed with the logo of a Marine unit which fought in Vietnam and nicknamed the "Walking Dead." He bought the lighter, and while he did not smoke, he sometimes thought about the Marine who might have carried it and whether or not he was still alive. But, today, Frank was with Marie-France, and although they were whiling away time together, they agreed that, if they were to find something small, something interesting and not too costly, they would purchase it and take it back to their little apartment along the Seine.

Before long, the two lovers found themselves in an area of the flea market where the more exquisite pieces of furniture, art work and antiques could be found. Antique lamps, canvases painted in oil and dating from past centuries, fine highly polished pieces of furniture and statues in bronze and marble of every height were on display. As they were passing one of the smaller stalls, Marie-France caught Frank by the arm and drew his attention to a small, beautifully rubbed and polished bronze statue of what seemed to be a nude, male, African eunuch. The statue was about two feet tall, and the figure was wearing only some kind of Egyptian headdress. From the statue, there seemed to be a radiance, a light coming from somewhere within the metal, and it emitted a strange, green glow. There were no visible sources of light, no electric cord running from its base, but, the glow was there, and its intensity seemed to increase in direct proportion to the distance between it and Marie-France. She stepped closer, and out of nowhere, bathed in the now more intense glow of the statue, an old man, perhaps the owner of the stall, appeared and said, "You like, mademoiselle?"

Startled by the sudden appearance of the antique seller, Marie-France said, *"Je la trouve interessant."* The old man had the face and hands of an eighty year old, but his eyes sparkled with a youthful exuberance. Marie-France continued in English by responding, *"Je...*I was looking at the light. I see no cord."

—No, it comes from the lights around the market. It reflects almost everything.

Frank stepped in and, noticing the interest Marie-France seemed to have for this strange statue, he said, *"C'est combien?"* The old man hesitated for a moment, then, looking at Marie-France, he asked, "It is for the lady?"

—Yes, I would like to buy it for her.

Frank looked at the young woman who, he had realized, had taken his heart. Marie-France smiled. The price Frank paid for the statue was lower than he had expected. But, the look on Marie-France's face when he said that he wanted to buy the statue for her would have made him go in debt for almost any amount. The shop keeper lifted the statue off its base and took it in the back of the stall for wrapping, and as he moved away from the young couple who had made the purchase, the glow from the statue seemed to diminish. Marie-France said, *"Mon amour,* are you sure?" Frank just smiled, lifted her hand to his lips and kissed it softly. He paid the old man, put the statue under one arm, and with the other, led Marie-France back to the metro and the two of them, no, the three of them, for the statue was the first item purchased for their apartment and now part of them, headed back to their little garret in the Latin Quarter.

Once back in their little hide-a-way along the Seine, Frank placed his package containing the statue he had purchased for Marie-France on the table along with the other items he had bargained for in the flea market. Among those other things were two lavender-scented candles. Frank imagined that the lavender in the candles had come from the flower which grows so profusely throughout Provence. Marie-France had busied herself by making a *salade nicoise*, and when she had finished, Frank cleared the table of his purchases, and he and his lover sat down to dinner where they shared a bottle of red wine and discussed their excursion to the *Marche aux puces.* Frank's French was better than Marie-France's English, but the conversation went back and forth in the two languages, and they laughed at each other's use their native idioms and accents.

When they had finished their meal, Frank lifted the dishes from the table and took them to the sink for washing. Then, he lit two of the candles he had purchased and turned off the lights to the apartment. In the light of the candles and with the soft glow of the neon lights coming from the Latin Quarter's restaurants and bistros, Frank stepped closer to Marie-France and put his arms around her softly. He kissed her neck, and said, "Je t'aime." Then, he walked over to the still unwrapped package sitting on the floor, picked it up and undid the paper surrounding it and placed it on the night stand near their bed. As if to admire her new gift, Marie-France approached and as she did, that same mysterious green glow seemed to emerge from the bronze itself. She and Frank both laughed knowing or at least thinking that light from the quarter below was reflecting off the highly polished metal. Then, from the small clothes closet, Frank took out one of the two metal folding chairs, only used when visitors would sometimes be invited for dinner. He unfolded the chair, placed it in the center of the bedroom and covered its back and seat with a soft, cotton blanket.

Marie-France just watched. She knew what he was doing. She had experienced her lover's expertise in such things previously. She knew that Frank would undress her slowly, lead her to the chair, seat her upon it, spread her legs tenderly and kneel in front of her...that he would tease her nipples with his tongue and lips, kiss her belly every so softly and then, repeat the same thing until she was wet with expectation...that he would lead her to his bed, tantalize her even further with his tongue which fluttered from one breast to the other like a butterfly drunk from the nectar of a thousand perfumed flowers, then, he would take her until she cried out waiting for her first climax to subside. Marie-France was not wrong. Everything she foresaw took place, but, there was one subtle difference. During the intensity of their lovemaking, Marie-France thought she noticed a more pronounced green glow emanating from the statue, and while she knew that the man inside her was her American lover, she sensed the presence of something or someone else close to her body, someone else in the room with them. The improbability of such a thing made her smile, and she relaxed even more. Then, she rode out her second climax, and she whispered in Frank's ear, "Tu me branches, mon amour."

Days later, while Frank explored the book stalls along the banks of the Seine looking for old prints or souvenirs relating to things he had studied or wanted to see, Marie-France would go to her work at the library, the *Bibliotheque Nationale*, wondering what had changed her life. She knew that Frank was scheduled to return to his teaching position in the United States. But, he had told her that he had fallen in love with her, that he did not want to leave her. She also knew that, while Frank was a true Francophile, he loved his own country very much. He had told her that most former Marines learn to love their country more than most Americans and that he loved teaching. Marie-France had a decision to make. She, too, had fallen in love, and she wanted this good looking, French speaking American to stay in her life.

Later that evening, when she arrived back at the apartment in the quarter, Frank had not yet returned. For some strange reason, perhaps thinking about Frank, she looked at the statue located on the night stand in her bedroom. Its glow was hardly discernible. But, when she moved closer, the greenish radiance seemed to increase. She hastily searched for some other source of light, perhaps coming from the street below. She found none. Tired of the inexplicable, she began removing her work clothes and decided to get into something more comfortable before dinner. Marie-France was about to discover more about this statue picked up in a flea market.

As Marie-France removed an article of clothing, the soft green light seemed to become more pronounced. Standing in front of the statue in only her bra and panties, she was drawn to it more out of interest than fear of the unknown. She unsnapped her bra and let it fall to the floor, and the statue almost sparkled. She shuddered. Then, she slipped her thumbs into the tops of her panties and slid them down her legs on to her ankles, and as she did so, the glow seemed to become more intense. Thinking that the silk sliding down her skin had produced some kind of static electricity, she sat down on the bed, leaned back on a pillow and smiled at her stupidity; such things do not take place in Paris.

Then, as if some far away voice was speaking to her, she thought that someone, Frank perhaps, was telling her to recline fully across the bed. She obeyed. The green glow seemed to rise up to the ceiling, hover over her, and then slowly encompass her entire body. Although impossible, she felt that the light had fingers, that it was massaging her body, intimately, and in a kind of spontaneity, she began to undulate in motion with the light which now bounced off the ceiling and onto the bed. She touched herself, but she felt that the spasm which arched her back and brought her to climax was not of her own doing. She immediately got up, and that is when she noticed, much to her own relief, that, just outside one of the windows of her apartment, down at street level, there was a green neon sign which read, "Bistro de Notre Dame", and next to that was the familiar green neon cross of a local pharmacy. Marie-France quickly took a shower.

When Frank returned that evening from his search among the *bouquinistes* along the Seine, he was carrying a few old books, a baguette and a nice fish wrapped in newspaper. He could never get over how the fish sellers wrapped their ware in yesterday's *journal*, but he did appreciate the thrift of such shopkeepers, and he knew that most of the French-schooled people, including fishmongers, were readers. Why waste a good newspaper? In the apartment, he laid down his purchases and looked at Marie-France. He noticed that her

59

face was flushed, and he asked her if she had just climbed the stairs ahead of him. She said, "Non, je suis contente de te voir", and she began preparing the fish Frank had brought home. Nothing more was said about the day's events that evening. They did not make love. Marie-France seemed preoccupied and tired, and they both had things to do the next day.

The next morning, Frank left early. He had some research and reading to do at the *Bibliotheque Nationale*, and he expected Marie-France to accompany him to the place where she worked. She mentioned that she was not feeling well and added that she would take one of her free days to arrange things in the apartment. Before he left, Marie-France put her arms around him, held him close, and said, "Frank, do you love me? Are you going to leave me?" Frank looked at her and responded, "Marie-France, there is a saying we use in the Marine Corps, 'The change is forever.' You have changed my life even more." He held her, kissed her and said that they would talk about everything when he returned that evening.

Frank didn't return until early evening. He had come across some interesting things Francois Villion had written in the 15th century, and some of these writings were in the author's own hand. To imagine having in front of him something written sometime in the 1400's was unbelievable, and he felt that, for the first time, he understood the poet's words. Finished with his work on the poet, Frank hurried home. As he entered the quarter, he looked up at his garret window on the top floor of his building. The window was open, and emanating from it was a soft green glow of light.

Frank climbed the stairs two at a time. He opened the door, headed for the bedroom and discovered Marie-France in the throws of ecstacy. She was lying nude on the bed, and her face was as flushed as it had been the day before. She wore a Mona Lisa like smile on her face, and she hardly noticed Frank now standing beside her bed. Frank sat down beside her, held her hand and asked if she was all right. She said yes, and the eerie glow which had filled the room when he had first entered seemed to dissipate as they talked. The statue, now lacking some of its luster, was beside her on the night stand. Nothing more was said. The young couple took their dinner by candle light, and they went to bed together with Marie-France holding Frank close. But, they did not make love.

The next morning when Frank awoke to the sounds of street cleaners and shopkeepers preparing for tourists, Marie-France was gone. Her clothes, the few well chosen and expensive outfits she had brought to the apartment, were also gone as was the statue which occupied the night stand beside their bed. A simple note was left lying on the table. It read, "Frank, I love you so much. I know you must leave, that you must return to the USA, and that you must not give up teaching—the job you love. I will love you always. Marie-France"

Frank quickly left the apartment. He first stopped at a little bistro directly outside the entrance to his building. He and Marie-France often stopped there before going their separate ways. There, while ordering a *café au lait* and croissant, he inquired with the waiter whether he had seen Marie-France that morning. No one at the bistro had seen her. Frank then went to the *Bibliotheque Nationale* where personnel at the library with whom Marie-France worked told Frank that they had not seen her at work for at least a week, that she had left no forwarding address, and that she had not given notice of leaving or returning.

Frank's summer stay in Paris was drawing to a close, but for the next two weeks, he looked for the woman who had totally changed his life. He went back to the flea market. He took his lunches at the <u>Bon Couscous</u> where they had first met and often went together days after that first meeting. The *maitre d'* whom Frank had befriended had not seen her lately, and when he checked back at the library, her place of work, there was still no word of anyone having seen her. Marie-France seemed to have vanished.

Near the end of August, when it came time for Frank's summer vacation to end, he made one of the biggest decisions of his life. Instead of returning to public school teaching in the United States, he would try to find the woman who had changed his life, the woman he loved. While the decision to remain in France was not made in haste, he knew that he would stay in Paris. After all, all he had to do was, instead of following the yellow brick road, he would walk the city at night and look for the soft glow of an errant virescence emanating from some open window. That soft green glow would perhaps point the way and assure that the change would be forever.

Chapter 2

The Decision

It had been done. Frank had decided to stay in France. There was no reason to return to a little town in the Allegheny Mountains of Western Pennsylvania. There was very little left for him there, and if necessary, he could find another teaching job in most states back home. Besides, and more importantly, the girl of his dreams had led him to give up his teaching position back in the states, and he wanted to know more about this young woman who had entered his heart and soul. What was it about Marie-France which had made Frank take such a step? In the days and weeks to come, Frank would ponder such questions, but he had other things to do before he could begin his search for the woman he loved.

Staying in France for more than six months required a visa, and he would need some way of making money. His garret apartment in the Latin Quarter of Paris was not too expensive, and he had mastered the art of eating well on little money, something he had learned from the French years ago as a young undergraduate student. Frank sat out to take care of these essential things immediately.

Frank determined that his first efforts should center around the visa and after obtaining that, he would arrange for a work permit. He went to the American Embassy just off the Concorde Square, spoke to the Marine guards there, traded some leatherneck stories with them, and got the necessary papers he needed to fill out for a visa and a temporary work permit. Being a former Marine helped him over some of the red tape most others would encounter, and he was thankful for the time he had given the Corps. Next, he went directly to the Cultural International Alliance, a private tour company whose specialty it was to arrange tours for American high school students and teachers while in France.

Frank had chaperoned such tours for his own students back home with the CIA, and the company had his file on record. That, as well as his excellent knowledge of France and Paris, his proficiency in French and English, and his willingness to give his all in everything he did, made Frank a perfect candidate for a tour guide for the CIA group in Paris. Almost immediately, the tour company gave Frank two weeks training in and around Paris. He learned more about the city's monuments, its churches, French history, and he toured all the museums he had not visited previously as a tourist and student. Years later, people doing the same job would have to pass strict exams concerning the things tourists would see in order to earn a tour guide's credentials. Frank mastered these requirements easily. After all, he was on a mission; he was looking for the woman he loved, and he needed this job to finance his search. Frank was hired almost immediately. His company was pleased with his excellent use of

French, and his experience in working with American teenagers would prove to be invaluable.

Within a short time, Frank's employers found him to be one of their top guides. His French was better than they had expected, his knowledge of Paris and its surroundings was superior to even some of the native born guides, some of whom were *provincial,* people not born and raised in Paris, and Frank's ability to meld with American and other English speaking high school and college students was excellent. Those students found Frank to be in sync with their likes and dislikes, and although he was strict in his demand that they get all that they had paid for as members of a tour group, he was understanding and considerate when it came time for them to have some fun. He told them the interesting stories about Napoleon, Marie-Antoinette, Louis XIV, and he even made the fictitious characters of Jean-Valjean, Quasimodo, the Count of Monte Cristo and Esmeralda come alive. In Frank, the CIA, his employer, had a winner. But, from time to time, Frank had some problems with American and English adult chaperones.

In most cases, American student groups taken to France are under the guidance of female chaperones, teachers and a few parents who want to see their sons and daughters enjoy a trip abroad, something they had never been able to do as students growing up in the 40's and 50's. Most teachers of French in the United States were women, not former Marines who grew up in the coal fields of Pennsylvania. Frank wondered why more men did not teach languages, but he never thought much about it until he became a tour guide. American teacher/chaperones were usually in their early 30's or 40's, rather attractive and very mindful of the students they had brought across the Atlantic. On occasion, however, some of these dutiful chaperones would be attracted to Frank, this good looking, young, former Marine who once taught French back in the United States.

Upon meeting his groups at the airport, Frank would take them by bus through the City of Lights to their hotel. Once they had checked in, Frank was required to stay at these hotels with his group. As part of his job during the students' stay in France, Frank was on call 24/7. During the day, on all the scheduled trips to museum, monuments and restaurants, Frank took care of tickets, explanations and special dietary demands. In the evening after dinner, he was pretty much free to do as he pleased, but he usually stayed close to the hotel.

It was the responsibility of the American chaperones to hold a curfew and make bed checks assuring that, for at least a certain time, the students were all in their assigned rooms. After bed check, usually at 11 P.M., the chaperones would get together, go over the days' events, confirm with Frank for the next day's itinerary, and then go to bed. One night, one of the chaperones, a beautiful young woman, Miss Collins, decided to pay Frank a visit after curfew and bed checks.

Frank had noticed Miss Collins, of course. She was what Frank called, "*bien tournee*", and in spite of another woman taking up most of Frank's

A Hint of Jasmine and Lavender
An Erotic Romance

thoughts on the matter, it was hard not
to be attracted to such a well developed
and pretty woman. Miss Collins had a
good speaking knowledge of the French
language, and she seemed to be very
dedicated to her students. During the
evening meals which everyone took
together as a group, she would often
pull up her chair next to Frank and talk
about what her students had seen
during the day.

One evening at dinner, Miss
Collins asked Frank if she could talk to
him about something after the students
had been checked into their rooms.
Being accommodating was part of
Frank's responsibilities, and he agreed

to meet with the teacher/chaperone, but he suggested that they meet at the hotel bar. That would be a good place to keep an eye on the front door of the hotel and make sure no student decided to go out for a midnight snack of pizza or worse, a glass of wine at some discotheque.

Later, at the hotel bar, Frank waited for Miss Collins and her co-chaperones to complete the rounds of her students' rooms. When she arrived at the bar, Frank saw that she had changed clothes. She was wearing shorts, a tee shirt and sandals. Other than Frank, the only other person there was the barman, and he admired what had just walked in. Frank ordered *un coup de rouge* for Miss Collins, and they moved to a table in one corner of the bar. The barman went about his business knowing that his input would not be necessary and perhaps not appreciated by the young lady who had just entered the bar.

At first, Miss Collins discussed the next day's itinerary. As she did so, she moved closer to Frank where he was seated, and she spread out on the table in front of him some maps of Pere Lachaise Cemetery and Montmartre. They discussed visiting the tombs of Edith Piaf, Moliere, the painter, Jacques-Louis David, Chopin and others

who had been buried there long before
Jim Morrison would take the interest of
those making pilgrimages to tombs of
their idols. Soon, Miss Collins'
questions began to get a little more
personal.

Her questions began innocently
enough. She wanted to know if Frank
was married, how long he had been in
France, where he had studied and what
made him remain in France instead of
continuing his career in public school
teaching. Frank answered all her
questions, and it was difficult not to
notice that she wore no bra, smelled of
a great perfume, and that she had
touched him several times on his arms

and hands when making a point on what they should do the next day. Then she said, "I have a nice bottle of French white burgundy in my room. Would you like to try it?" Frank smiled appreciatively, and he declined by first thanking her profusely. He then told her truthfully that he admired her attention to her students. Then he did something he did not like to do; he lied. He said that his company, the CIA, would not allow guides to enter the room of any chaperones. He did not bring up the fact that he had just lost the woman who meant more to him than life itself, that he was still in love with her, and that he was still looking for her. He got up from the table, gently lifted one of the chaperone's hands to his lips, softly pressed his lips to it, and said, "Your confidence and trust in me is very much appreciated. Now, I must get some sleep if I am to give you my best tomorrow." He courteously escorted Miss Collins back to her room and the two of them went to their separate beds.

Once Frank had finished getting ready for bed, had laid out all his information he would need for the next day's tours and visits and arranged the clothing he would wear the next morning, he crawled into his single bed and stared at the ceiling. He thought back to how he had made love to Marie-France back in their garret overlooking the Latin Quarter. He played over in his mind how he had aroused her, how she had mounted him as he lay back on their bed. She would pull his hands toward her breasts, and once there, he would cup them with both hands while his thumb and forefingers lightly pinched and caressed her nipples. Lifting herself up, she would then guide him inside her and wait for him to slide his hand down across her belly in order to allow his middle finger to slide in and on her clitoris. With her on top, Frank and Marie-France would hook their legs so as to make two bodies become one, and as she moved her body up and down on his, she allowed his finger and penis to coax her to climax. Once her breathing had returned to normal, Frank would help Marie-France change positions with him, slip into her again and explode inside her as she reached her second orgasm. Then, the two lovers would fall asleep next to each other in a soft green light emanating from somewhere close to their bed. Thinking about Marie-France helped Frank forget what might have transpired had he accepted Miss Collins' invitation to share a bottle of wine with her in her room, and he fell asleep knowing that his next day's work, showing students

85

the beauties and mysteries of France would perhaps lead him to the woman he loved.

Chapter 3

The Search

The next day, Frank concluded his tour, said his goodbyes to Miss Collins and her students, and accepted a gift from the entire group. In a little bag, Frank later found a good number of French francs and a bottle of white burgundy. He then returned to the CIA office, turned in his papers and collected his salary. He was given the dates for his next assignment, and he went to a bistro in the Latin Quarter were, over a Pelforth *brune,* he laid out plans in his search for Marie-France.

Frank knew that Marie-France had worked in the *Bibliotheque Nationale,* the largest and most prestigious library in France.   Her family name was Gagnon, and she had told him that she did have a brother living in Provence in the south of France. He had a picture of Marie-France. In the picture, she was standing alone in front of a sculpture by Rodin. The sculpture was his *Penseur,* The Thinker, and it was located at the Musee Rodin at Hotel Biron in the Rue de Varenne. That museum would be the point of departure in his search for Marie-France.

Between educational tours, each guide at the CIA had two weeks off, and on his first day away from work, Frank arrived early at the Musee Rodin where, among those who were admiring the works of the famous French sculptor, Frank would begin his search for Marie-France. He had chosen Sunday for his visit to the museum since Marie-France had that day off when she worked at the library. He arrived promptly at 10 A.M., and he went directly to the outside gardens where Rodin's *Thinker* was on view. Frank stood in front of the sculpture and positioned himself where he thought the person who took Marie-France's picture would have been standing. He tried to make his former love materialize before him, and in his mind's eye, he could see her clearly. Smiling back at him, or at the taker of the photo, Marie-France was radiant. The picture had been taken during the summer months, and it was recent enough that even the clothes she wore were familiar to Frank. Then, something broke his reverie.

Just at the moment at which he thought he could reach out and touch the ethereal image in front of him in the photo gallery of his mind, one of the visitors of the museum passed in front of him and erased the conjured up image of Marie-France. Frank looked around at his fellow visitors and decided to go inside where some of the most expressive works of Rodin were found. As he entered the ground floor, he was met by creations of figures emerging from bronze and blocks of white marble. Immensely striking, vital and life-like, Rodin's sculptures mesmerized those who looked upon them. Frank was especially taken with one of the works, *Le Baiser.* Known as *The Kiss* by speakers of English, the statue portrayed two lovers, a man and woman, who were totally nude and seated side by side on a rock. The woman has her left arm around her lover's neck, and she has exposed and offered up to her lover her nakedness. The man, in his embrace, has placed his right hand on his lover's thigh, and his thumb is pointed upward toward the woman's breast as if to point out the final destination of his hand. The two, locked together for eternity, seemed to epitomize what Frank had hoped he would have had with Marie-France. While he and Marie-France had been in the same position from time to time, and while they could have posed for the great sculptor, only the memory of such things was all that was left of what was once a moment in time.

Shocked back into reality by the solidity of the white marble and its unmoving and eternal state, Frank stepped back and wiped a tear from his eye, and as he did so, a voice said to him, *"Monsieur se souvient de quelque chose?"* A beautiful, well-dressed young woman was standing in front of him, and her concern for Frank seemed genuine. Frank quickly regained his composure and said, *"Oh, non, mademoselle, c'est un petit rhume de cerveau, c'est tout."* The woman smiled and walked on wishing that the handsome young man she just spoke to had told the truth.

After lunch, Frank came back to the museum, spent a few hours walking through the gardens in the hope that what had inspired Marie-France to pose in the past in front of Rodin's statue would bring her back again. Frank knew that he had to move on, and for the next few days, he went to every library in Paris and asked if Marie-France Gagnon had applied for work. No such person was on staff in any of the places he searched, and when shown the photo of Marie-France taken at the Rodin Museum, none of the employees recognized her.

Frank walked the streets at night in many of the student quarters for the next two weeks, and his gaze often wandered up at the top floors of the typical three or four story buildings that made up much of the Parisian skyline in the hope that he would catch sight of the flicker of some strange, green light. But, all that he was able to distinguish was the reflection of the familiar green neon cross of a local pharmacy. It was now time to go back to work as a tour guide. He made his way back to his garret apartment along the Seine where, after he had arranged his things for the next day, he made love once more to Marie-France in his mind.

Chapter 4

Perfume

Within days, Frank had welcomed another group of American college students and their chaperones who had booked a tour taking in the wonders of southern France. The group, thirty students and three chaperones, departed Paris and made their way south toward the *midi*, the word used in reference to the south of France. Along the way, Frank focused the group on the small city of Chartres, and he gave them a tour of the cathedral, a jewel of Gothic architecture built during the twelfth and thirteenth centuries. He took the students into the crypt and pointed out what many Christians believe to be the original veil worn by the mother of Christ. Frank was careful to point out that this was only the official view of certain Christians and that the students themselves would have to determine whether or not the veil on display was authentic. Some students, especially those of the Jewish faith, showed their appreciation for his candor by smiling. One of them even winked in his direction. The teacher/chaperones nodded in agreement, and the Catholics in the group took in every one of Frank's words and sorted them out in their own way.

After lunch, the group, made up of more young women than young men, continued on toward Tours, a larger city where they would spend the night. The entire group had dinner that evening at the *Chanteclair*, a restaurant located in the center of Tours where, it is said, the best French spoken in France can be heard. Most of the students and all of the chaperones consumed much of the *vin du pays*, wine made in the Loire

Valley. Even Frank had one glass with which he toasted the group's positive frame of mind. However, a few of the young students became too positive, and Frank helped the chaperones escort them back to the hotel while those who had imbibed much less were allowed to explore the city in small groups. Later, Frank stayed up with the chaperones, all women very properly dressed and well organized who admired their young American guide. Frank waited for all the students to return to the hotel before he retired for the night. He fell asleep thinking about Marie-France.

The next day after breakfast, Frank's group was on its way toward the south of France. As the bus made its way along roads lined with plane trees and oaks, Frank pointed out the big green balls of mistletoe, the parasite which lives off the trees lining the road. He related stories about the little towns through which they passed, and he spoke about the historic chateaux which line the major route running through the Loire Valley. Frank also thought about Marie-France and where she might have gone. As he watched the plane trees rush by outside the bus window, he wondered what she might be doing and whether she still had the little statue he had given her, the only thing she took other than her clothes. Frank knew that his life would not be complete without seeing Marie-France again. He needed to know what had made her leave so abruptly, and he desperately needed her to know that he loved her.

The student tour group passed through Bourges, and its medieval buildings still intact gave evidence of a magnificent past. Next came the city of Le Puys with buildings clinging to the sides of cliffs as if they had made an effort to escape the stress and strain of modern life and had climbed up and away from the fast-paced life below. Finally, after more than several hours ride, the group arrived at Le Pont du

Gard, the ancient Roman aqueduct still used today as a bridge for cars, trucks and pedestrians who want to cross the river Gard running underneath.

The small village which sets next to the aqueduct would serve as a point of departure for the next day's tour, but before retiring for the night, Frank made sure that all the students got the chance to cross the aqueduct on foot, take a few pictures with flash and make it back to the hotel before midnight. Frank was not besieged by any of the good looking young ladies or any of the attractive female chaperones during the night, and he was glad everyone seemed to be businesslike and interested in what he had to show them. The next day's activities, however, would challenge his very soul and test his feelings for Marie-France.

The next morning, after croissants and café au lait, the group set off for a small village nestled on the top of a promontory overlooking the fields of flowers grown for the perfumeries which were abundant in the region. The village was noted for its market place filled with flowers grown in the region, fruits and vegetables common to that part of France, and the many stalls from which the local inhabitants sold souvenirs to the tourists who came from all over the world. Besides seeing a rural, agricultural village which had held to its tradition of allowing no motor vehicles in its main square, the students would be able to see the little town during one of its market days when everyone from miles around came to barter and supply themselves with their weekly needs. But, the biggest source of attraction was the perfumes sold in the open market. Flowers grown locally made their way to the perfume factories in the area, and the local populace had their own homemade varieties of perfumes which sold for hundreds of dollars more in Paris. Here in this mountain village, one could purchase the same scents sold in and around the Rue Royale for one third the price. After an explanation of what could be had, meeting times for departure had been made, and how to barter with the townspeople had been outlined, the students went their separate ways in search of purchases which would either please themselves or someone they loved. Frank set out on his own, too.

The market place was filled with tourists, merchants and townspeople from miles around. It was a beautiful, warm day, and the opened stalls offered leather goods, flowers of all colors and scents, fruit and vegetables, ceramics and souvenirs emblazoned with the emblems of various kings and officialdom from the region. The rays of the sun seemed to shine into the center of the market place as if it was a giant spotlight illuminating a Hollywood movie set. It would not have surprised Frank if Catherine Deneuve or Fanny Ardent suddenly appeared as if ready to make a scene for some *film noir*. Everyone seemed happy, and Frank was pleased that many of his group's students had already purchased things which would make their trip to France memorable.

Frank continued along through the crowded market place and decided to turn down a little street running perpendicular to the main square. He found himself in front of a little stall where bottles of many colored liquids were laid out on a table for display. A very handsome, older woman was seated behind the table, and she was wearing an attractive and revealing light summer dress adorned with flowers. She noticed that she had attracted Frank's attention, and she offered, *"Monsieur cherche quelque chose pour une femme?"* Embarrassed that his gaze was so obvious, Frank responded that she had been right; he was looking for something for a woman.

The woman stood up as though she wanted to give Frank a better view of not only what she was selling but of herself as well. Although ten or more years older than Frank, this woman was not only beautiful, her body seemed molded for the clothing she wore, and her dress perfectly outlined and embraced her breasts, stomach and hips. Her face was make up free, beautiful and bursting with good health assisted by what Frank supposed was good country living. Her all-knowing smile gave Frank the impression that she knew that he liked what he saw in front of him, and then she asked what it was that he might have in mind...for purchase.

Frank told the woman that he would like a perfume for a beautiful woman, a woman whose skin was as soft as the petals of flowers he had seen in the market place, a perfume which, when touched to her skin, would mix with the woman's natural oils and excite a man to kneel in front of her and proclaim his love for her. Such a request seemed to impress the perfume seller, and she had Frank try a few samples of her perfumes by putting just a slight essence on the back of her wrists. One of the samples and its scent burst in on that part of Frank's brain which held the memory of Marie-France. Like the petite madeleine dunked in a cup of tea by Marcel Proust's character in *A la Recherche du Temps Perdu,* the taste of which had conjured up a moment in time from the past, the perfume Frank had just sampled had the same effect; it was the same scent worn by Marie-France, jasmine and lavender, and with the slightest essence of this perfume, the thought of Marie-France rushed into his mind. He knew that he would have to have it, and he told the woman standing in front of him that he would take several bottles.

That the perfume seller liked Frank was evident. She took the time to go into her home behind her stall to look for some colored paper appropriate for wrapping the gift. No other perfume seller would have done this at market. Purchases made there were simply handed over to the buyer who put them into a *filet*, the little net-like bag carried by most French shoppers. Frank waited outside. Soon, the woman appeared at the doorway of her home and motioned for him to come inside. She mentioned that he should pick out the paper.

Once inside, Frank admired the quaint but well appointed and decorated interior of the woman's home. Frank stood in the kitchen where, laid out on a table, were several pieces of delicate wrapping paper. The woman pointed to them, and Frank picked out a soft, lavender tissue paper. The woman smiled her approval, and she began to carefully cover the perfumes, and as she was doing so, she asked Frank if he knew the proper way to give a woman perfume. Frank admitted that he had no idea that there was such a thing. She then asked if he would like to know. Frank said yes, and the perfume seller motioned for him to follow her into the next room, her bedroom.

Hesitatingly, Frank followed the attractive, French perfume seller into her bedroom. She went over to her dressing table, picked up a small bottle of her own perfume and said, "I want you to think that you have just brought me a gift, this perfume. I want you to believe that it is a perfume you would like me to wear." Frank nodded his comprehension. She continued, "You must know that, in France, if a man buys the woman he loves perfume, he has earned the privilege of putting that perfume wherever he wants on the woman's body. Do you understand?" Frank again nodded his understanding. Then, after handing the bottle of perfume to Frank, she said, "Take this, and practice on me."

The perfume seller stepped back, lifted her arms over her head, slipped off her dress and let it fall behind her on the floor. She was outstandingly beautiful, and Frank knew immediately why she wore nothing underneath her dress. Her body was beautifully proportioned, and it needed no cosmetic support or enhancement. Such a body made Frank think of the white marble statues he had witnessed in the Rodin Museum. The woman's breasts were almost as perfect as those of Marie-France, and they betrayed no evidence of ever having been restrained by a bra. Her belly was smooth and flat and led into her thighs with a sensual curve highlighted by a neatly trimmed area of pubic hair. She was stunning. She raised her arms again and put her hands behind her head offering her entire body for his experimentation and said, *"Alors?"*

Frank looked at what she had offered him, and his eyes lingered for a short time on her gifts. Then, he opened the bottle of perfume she had handed him. He dabbed some of the essence on his right index finger and moved closer to his now ready canvas of living flesh. Very carefully, allowing only one finger to come in contact with the woman's body, Frank bent down in front of her and applied the faintest amount of the perfume to the creases in the woman's skin behind her knees. He did the same to the backs of her ankles before he raised up and again looked into her eyes. Taking again only a small amount of the bottle's contents, and in using the same finger, Frank applied more of the fragrance to the area just below each of the woman's breasts. She quivered slightly when he did so.

Frank then asked the woman to turn her back to him, and with her hands still above her head, she turned around slowly. Frank took a little more of the perfume, and using the same soft brush which was his finger, he traced the middle of her lower back. He did the same to the folds of soft skin running under the woman's arm pits. Then, he screwed the top back on the bottle, breathed in the faint fragrance of the perfume which now had mixed with the natural oils of the woman's body, put the bottle down, moved in closer behind his living canvas and whispered in the woman's ear, "Madame, votre beaute est aussi etonnante que le parfum. Merci, mille fois." Having given the woman a sincere compliment and thanks, Frank turned, picked up his purchases he had left in the woman's kitchen, and he walked out the door into the sunlight still streaming down through the trees into the main square of the village. He joined some of the students still milling around the marketplace, and they all made their way back to the bus.

That afternoon, as the group headed back to the hotel near the Pont du Gard, Frank reminisced. He let his mind race over the things that he had seen and learned that afternoon. In the buzz of the students' discussion of what they had purchased in the market, Frank wondered to himself why he had not used the entire bottle of perfume in his experimentation. Then, he knew why. The woman was not Marie-France.

Chapter 5

Free Time

As soon as Frank and his student group returned to Paris from their trip to the south of France, Frank was given another two weeks off before he had to accept his next assignment. On the very day he got back to his little garret apartment overlooking the Latin Quarter, he went through his mail and prayed for messages from Marie-France.

119

Nothing. He then sat down and sketched out a plan which, he hoped, would lead him to rediscover the woman he loved or at least learn the reason for her strange disappearance.

First, Frank decided to scour once again all the libraries in Paris. Marie-France had worked in the *Bibliotheque Nationale,* and he hoped that her work in such a prestigious institution would land her a job in a similar workplace. At the same time, he would haunt all the favorite spots that he and Marie-France had admired when they were together, places such as Montmartre, the Champs-Elysees and the café, Georges V, the flea market at Clignoncourt, the

Rodin Museum, the Pere Lachaise Cemetery, and of course, the Latin Quarter and their favorite restaurant, *Le Bon Couscous.*

On his first night back from his latest tour, as he lay in his bed, Frank contemplated all the things he would say to Marie-France when they next met, and he was sure he would see her again. He would tell her how much he had missed her, that his thoughts were punctuated with the firm belief that he would find her, that he knew that they should be together, and that he wanted to spend the rest of his life with her. He would not ask why she had left him so abruptly, where she had been or what she had been doing. Frank's only hope was that he would find her again, that she would see and feel the sincerity in his words to her. As her face faded with his thoughts, he fell asleep.

When he awoke the next morning, Marie-France's face was still etched on his mind. Frank showered, got dressed and went downstairs and out on to the street to a little bistro where he ordered and consumed his café au lait and croissants. While he drank his coffee, he made plans for the day, and first on his agenda would be the trips to the local libraries. At each one, Frank would show a picture of Marie-France standing in front of the Rodin statue and ask whether any such person had applied for a job. Next, he would spend the afternoon checking out places where he and Marie-France had enjoyed each other's company. Later, in the evening, he would patrol various quarters where the less fortunate had taken apartments, and he would look up at windows on the top floors hoping to catch sight of a strange green glow of light flickering through the glass from inside.

By noon that same day, Frank had come up empty in his search at the main desk of more than several libraries. No one had seen or knew the girl in the photo Frank showed, but several young librarians, all males, took their time looking over the picture of the beautiful girl standing in front of one of Rodin's statue. One of these men offered, *"Bien tournee comme il faut!"*, but Frank's facial expression stopped any further comment on the girl's anatomy, and he quickly handed the photo back to Frank knowing that further indiscretion in any reference to the subject in the photo might result in a serious confrontation. Frank took a quick lunch, and headed out for the familiar haunts he and Marie-France had encountered together.

Frank's first stop was the Pont Neuf, the oldest bridge in Paris. The

Vert-Galant Square was found at the foot of the steps leading down from the street surface of the bridge, and on this little piece of land, adorned with a well manicured lawn and a few trees, was the statue of Henri IV, a Protestant turned Catholic in order to become king and killed by an assassin in 1610. This little square at the base of the bridge and close to the river was a favorite spot of lovers who, while watching *bateaux mouches* passing by on the waters, would express their love in long embraces and share their intimacy with onlookers riding the tourists boats. Frank and Marie-France had shared such things many times, and standing at the base of the statue, Frank imagined that he was once again holding the woman he loved, that he could feel her firm body with his hands, that his lips were on hers, and that such a moment in time could have been the subject of one of Paul Almasy's famous black and white photographs. Frank's reverie was broken by a young man who said, *"Monsieur, vous avez du feu?"* Somewhat startled, Frank responded by saying, *"Non, fume pas."*, and he walked away from the man who needed a light and walked back up the stairs and onto the bridge.

Frank caught a bus which crossed the *Seine* and made its way around the

Place de la Concorde and up the Champs-Elysees. When the bus had reached the area of the Arch of Triumph, Frank got off and walked to the Georges V, a little bistro which had a covered patio jutting out on to the walkway. There, he took a seat at a little round table, ordered a tea with lemon and sat back and observed the public walking by on the streets of the largest avenue in Paris.

It is said that, if you wait long enough at one of these little cafes which line the Champs-Elysees, you will eventually see someone from your hometown walk by. Frank had hardly expected to see someone from a little coal town in Pennsylvania walk by him in Paris, but, in the first months in the French capital, he did see one of his old and most respected professors, Mr. Van Horn, stroll by. Frank had called out to him, and the former student and his teacher talked for hours. Now, however, on these crowded streets in the heart of the City of Light, no one seemed to resemble anyone he had ever seen. There were many beautiful women who served as receptionists, sellers, managers and representatives of the Mercedes, Ferrari and Jaguar agencies located on this, the most beautiful avenue in Paris. Their were Arabs in native headdress, Africans in their tribal costumes, men of all ages dressed in Armani and blue jeans. Older women, dressed to the nines, taking their dogs for a stroll and not bothering to pick up their feces when their pets had defecated on the sidewalk, were seen among the hundreds of tourists from every country in the world. It was easy to pick out the Japanese loaded down with their Nikon cameras. The Americans, most of whom were chewing gum and wearing baseball caps, brushed elbows with women wearing saris and men in homburgs. And then, Frank let his eyes drift from the flow of people going by to the signs and marquees which were affixed to the sides of most buildings.

Frank's eyes scanned the facades of the boutiques and shops within his view. Something caught his eye. Located close to the entrance of the office of Dom Perignon, the famous champagne maker, was a bronze plaque on which, in gold letters, was, "Monsieur Geffroy Gagnon—Gerant". The name, "Gagnon" was like "Smith" in the United States, and Frank knew that he would see many more such names on doors, signs and building facades in his search for the woman with the same last name. Frank took another tea and spent another hour watching the sea of humanity undulate in its ebb and flow from one shop and café to another. But, the woman for whom Frank had been searching was not among this flotsam of human cargo passing by, and at afternoon's end, Frank made his way back to the Latin Quarter, showered and made plans for the evening.

Just before dark, Frank left his apartment overlooking the *Seine* and the street scene below, and he made his way via the metro to an area around Montmartre. He climbed the stairs leading up to the Basilica of Sacre Coeur, and walked the narrow streets lined with two and three-story buildings. Every so often, Frank would look up at

A Hint of Jasmine and Lavender
An Erotic Romance

the upstairs windows and hope to see an eerie green glow emanating from one of them. Part of him did not want to see such a thing. He wondered what such a light might mean, and he did not want his former lover to be in anyone's grasp but his own. After all, he was former Marine, and most guys like him did not believe in the supernatural; too much reality and experience had erased any possibility of such things happening. Frank's search ended around midnight. He made his way back down the hill from Montmartre and through the crowded streets near the Moulin Rouge toward the entrance to the metro. Along his way, Frank had to wave off several proposals made to him from several *belles de nuit* who pouted when he said, *"Non, merci."* Frank jumped the last metro train headed for the *rive gauche*, and before long, he was in his garret above the still bustling tourist and student quarter where, saddened by his lack of success in finding Marie-France, he fell into a deep but welcomed sleep.

Chapter 6

The Sighting

Frank's routine in the following days was similar to the day before. He visited more libraries, frequented the favorite haunts he and Marie-France had come to love, and, at night, he walked the quiet little streets bordered by small hotels and apartment buildings. Frank did this for more than several days without any success. Then, deciding to prepare for his next tour group, he went to the cathedral located in St. Denis.

Few tourists know what a perfect historic and significant monument can be found at St. Denis. Located at about a fifteen minute ride on the metro, the Paris suburb of St. Denis is just north of the French capital. The community of St. Denis got its name from the 3rd century Christian priest and first bishop of Paris who, it is said, was martyred by the romans who then controlled the city. St. Denis, so the story goes, was beheaded by the Romans in Montmartre, and that well known Parisian district reflects in its name the place of martyrdom. At the time of the beheading, the Christian priest is said to have bent down, picked up his head and walked the ten or so miles to the present site of the village of St. Denis. The martyr's Christian followers built a small church on the spot where the martyr fell, and in the 12th century, the first Gothic cathedral in Europe was built on the sacred burial site of St. Denis himself. It is this cathedral which is the site most tourists miss in their visits to Paris. While the cathedral itself is important from the standpoint of architecture, its contents are of equal interest.

Frank had learned that, from the time of Saint Louis in the 13th century, the French had wanted to establish a depository for the bodies of all the kings and queens who had reigned up to that time as well as for those who would follow.   Every king and queen from Clovis, the 5th century king who united the French kingdom to Marie-Antoinette, headless of course, rest inside the cathedral at St. Denis.

More importantly, the cadavers of the royalty were placed in ossuary which were sculpted into the likeness each held at death.   These sculptures are so perfect that the viewer can get a very good idea of what the dead king and queen looked like at the very moment of their death.   While no cameras had yet been invented, these pictures in stone have drawn thousands of tourists and historians over the years.

In this Rodin-like cemetery of French royalty at St. Denis, one can gaze upon statues of Louis XIV, the Sun King; Clovis; the mother of Charlemagne; Francois I, the king who brought Leonardo de Vinci to France in 1515; Henri IV; Louis XVI and his queen, Marie-Antoinette, both headless; and many others. The statues inside the cathedral at St. Denis represent a collection of some of the best sculptures in the world, but, there is a scratch on the smooth surface of all this history; no bodies can be found inside the sarcophagi of most kings and queens buried in this repository.

During the early days of the French Revolution, the French people ripped open the caskets and emptied all the bones in a common pit outside the church. Later, under the Restoration, these remains were uncovered and deposited in the crypt of the cathedral. The only bodies which remain intact in any of the sarcophagi are those of Louis XVI and his wife, Marie-Antoinette, and these bodies are without their heads which were thrown to the crowd watching the guillotining in the Place de la Concorde during the early days of the

A Hint of Jasmine and Lavender
An Erotic Romance

Revolution. Frank knew that such gory information would be well received by students who were tired of seeing so many churches during their tour; the fantastic serves to hold the interest of most teenagers. Here, in this historic, Gothic cathedral, the depository for famous French royalty, among the dead, Frank would continue his search for the living. He would hope to encounter Marie-France.

Frank knew that Marie-France loved sculpture and that she was especially fond of works which inspired long lasting love. If any statuary inspired such things, it might be the marble effigies of Francois I and his

140

queen, Claude of France or Catherine de Medici and her husband, Henri II, all of whom are naked with joined hands in the museum of funerary sculpture. It was a long shot, but his research at St. Denis needed to be done for his next tour group. All this and more occupied Frank's mind as the train pulled into the metro station at St. Denis.

When you initially step off the train at St. Denis, the cathedral cannot be seen. Signs pointing to the church and monument lead you through an outdoor market, past the city hall and out onto the open square which spreads out before you as would a giant cement carpet leading up to the massive Gothic structure. The cathedral's architecture betrays its early Gothic beginnings. Its size hints of later and more beautiful features such as the flying buttresses seen at Notre Dame in Paris. At St. Denis, this first Gothic cathedral is more related to Roman architecture characterized by great, round arches and barrel vaults which do not allow for the beautiful stained glass found in later churches. But, it was the inside which intrigued many historians and tourists, for here was a parade of the past kings and queens of France frozen in time by marble.

Frank went inside with some church goers and tourists. Services are still held near the entrance of the cathedral while the interior and the crypt can only be reached by purchasing a museum ticket which allows you to see up close and personal the magnificent sculptures and to descend into the crypt where the bodies of Marie-Antoinette and her husband lie, side by side, in red marble sarcophagi.

Frank bought his ticket and moved along with the flow of others into the area of the transept. There, he passed by the tombs of Charles Martel, Charlemagne's grandfather, and Berthe *au grand pied,* "Big foot Bertha", Charlemagne's mother. The funerary sculpture of this last mentioned person gave good reason why this woman had been given the moniker, "Big foot". One foot of the reclining figure in marble was indeed bigger than the other, and it had been polished smooth by visitors over the last hundred years.

Frank was just about to smile at the thought of servants making comments behind the back of Charlemagne's mother in some far off castle when he noticed a familiar shape moving away from him and out toward the exit at the front of the cathedral. The physical appearance of the young woman, even at such a distance, was unmistakable. Even with the clothing she wore, Frank was able to discern the fully feminine form of Marie-France, and in spite of the fact that signs everywhere in the cathedral read, *"Silence, s'il vous plait!"* Frank called out her name, "Marie-France!". The now unmistakable figure turned toward the person who called her name, seemed to recognize him, and then moved out quickly through the exit and into the crowd standing in front of the cathedral. The figure was indeed Marie-France.

Frank did his best to move through the museum/mausoleum filled with visitors who were now expressing facial displeasure with the young man who had broken the vow of silence in this hallowed place. In spite of the wrath he had earned from these onlookers, Frank made his way swiftly to the cathedral's exit and stood on its steps searching for some glimpse of Marie-France. It had started to rain, and the sea of umbrellas which sheltered the crowd in front of the cathedral also prevented Frank from picking out Marie-France from others. While he searched, Marie-France slipped out of the teaming mass of visitors and market goers and made her way to the metro platform where she caught a departing train toward Paris.

Frank searched in vain, and he asked himself why she had run. What made her reject him? She had been so close to him. Hadn't she heard him? He even thought he had seen her smile for a brief moment before she exited the cathedral and slipped away into the crowd outside. That smile, however so brief, was all that he needed to propel him on in his quest to rediscover the woman who had taken his heart. With renewed enthusiasm, Frank made his way into the crowd of umbrellas held by so many shoppers and tourists, and he scanned each face hoping to resurrect the sight he had seen inside the cathedral. After a while, he decided on making a more thorough search. That would come later, but he knew now that he would find her.

Chapter 7

"Bar Americain"

By the time Frank got down the cathedral steps and into the sea of humanity making its way through the market stalls and walkways, he knew that he would not be able to catch up to Marie-France. Frank was not even sure that she had seen him in the darkened interior of the cathedral, but, she did turn toward him and acknowledged her name when he called to her. Could she have recognized his voice? If she did, why would she have made her way out of the church so quickly and into the crowd? He tried to answer those questions as he made his way through the tarp-covered market stalls. As he searched for the face he loved in the mass of shoppers and tourists, Frank stopped briefly at one clothing stall and bought a rain slicker. He put it on and ventured back out into the little streets of the area surrounding the cathedral. He searched for an hour before giving up. He then returned to the metro station and waited for the next train. While waiting, Frank felt an excitement which came from his first sighting of Marie-France since she had left. On his way back to Paris, he fine tuned his plans which, he hoped, would bring him face to face with the woman he loved.

Frank still had a week before he was scheduled to pick up his next student group. He stuck to his search in walking at night through the areas around Montmartre and the Marais district, an area known for its low rent housing. He strolled down the Boul Mich where students and low income earners found cheaper places to live. He looked up in vain at windows through which he hoped to catch a glimpse or a flicker of green light knowing, too, that such a discovery might make him question whether his search might end with something he did not want to see. That antique statue still bothered him, but Frank quickly decided that the supernatural was not something his mind would accept, and he dismissed the thought immediately.

Frank spent the next few days in Montmartre near the Place Pigalle. In that area, you can always find a lot of bars, bistros and little street entrance hotels which cater to the street people, cross dressers, prostitutes and scam artists as well as to the few tourists who were not aware of what the well known area offered. The area around

Pigalle had a bad reputation, and Marie-France took Frank there just to point out its peculiarities. That's why he returned to such a place.

The walkways and streets were always busy, but they came alive at night. Crowded with *"belles de nuit"* and *"belles de jours"*, women who worked during the day as prostitutes and then went back to their children and husbands at the end of the work day. The clientele who catered to these working girls were usually the unsavory types who wanted to sample the life which existed in this area. Frank encountered men and women from every nation, soldiers, sailors, even some Marines. There were youth strung out on drugs and the down-and-out looking for someone to anchor them to the safety net of a hot meal and a free night's lodging. As he walked along Rue Blanche, Frank spotted a little bar with a neon sign displaying in big red letters, *"Bar Americain"*. Frank should have known better to go in, but in he went.

Most Americans know, and Frank was soon to learn, that an advertisement such as *"Bar Americain"* usually means high prices, underworld characters and scam artists ready to take advantage of any English speaking patron seeking either someone with whom to speak English or trying to find

153

a little piece of home in some far off place. But, for Frank, something told him that there might just be someone who had seen or who might know the woman whose picture he held in one hand as he entered the bar.

As soon as he entered, a curvaceous, buxom blond grabbed him by the arm and led him to a table in one dark corner of the dimly lit interior. As she walked Frank to the table, the girl asked him his name, welcomed him to the place and asked what he wanted to drink, and she did all this in French, not English. Frank liked the idea of not using English, and he ordered a *coup de rouge*, hoping to get a glass of nice

Bordeaux red which he would drink while making plans for the next day.

The young, blond woman left Frank and went to the bar for his drink. When she returned with his red wine, she also had a glass of expensive champagne for herself. Frank's education was about to become diverse. Although he knew that it was unlikely to encounter Marie-France in such a place, Frank decided to enjoy the wine which, as it turned out, was not bad, and he decided to practice his French with the girl who was now sitting at his table. He put Marie-France's picture in his pocket. Some degree of trust would have to be established before Frank could start asking questions about Marie-France.

The young woman who had welcomed Frank to this American bar was working for tips. She would greet unsuspecting guests to the establishment, make conversation with them, drink watered down champagne, and from time to time, offer to take the client to a nearby hotel where, for a price, they would make love. The woman was pretty and well built, and when she sat down at the table next to Frank, her breasts almost spilled out of the top of her dress like soup overflowing the rim of a bowl, and this soup looked especially good. Frank immediately made an effort to curb his appetite, and he started a conversation by asking the woman her name.

She told Frank that her name was Jasmine, that she was a native Parisian, that she worked at *Printemps,* one of the largest department stores in Paris, and that she was looking for a roommate. Frank doubted that the woman's name was Jasmine, although her perfume seemed to confirm that name and scent were the same. He noticed an accent which gave her away as being *meridionale,* an inhabitant of southern France, and he thought that she was a full-time employee of the *"Bar Americain"*; such a position required

157

long hours, and if you were pretty enough, as was Frank's cocktail waitress, a "working girl" would make more here than in a department store, at least while her youth and beauty lasted.

As she talked, Frank looked at this bar girl whose beauty and body probably earned her enough to live well in Paris. That she was looking for a roommate as she had said was a given. Frank was determined that the taker would not be him, and he continued the conversation by asking Jasmine, or whatever her name was, whether she had ever seen the young woman in the photo he held out to her. Jasmine took one look, and

158

with a devious smile, she said, "Yes, monsieur. She comes in here a little after ten o'clock every night." Frank blinked in amazement, and asked, "Why? With whom?" The girl smiled back and laughingly answered, "She works here. She is the mistress of the man behind the bar."

Frank just shook his head, and in a very sincere tone, he said, "That, mademoiselle, is not funny." Frank had seen the overweight, balding man behind the bar when he came in. That same man had been glaring at him since his arrival in the bar, and he motioned to Jasmine that she should drink up. Following the barman's silent orders, she did so, and Frank allowed himself to explore her features in greater detail.

Jasmine, his hostess in the bar, was rather pretty. Her decolletage revealed just enough to invite one's stare into its depths. Frank caught himself looking in that direction, and he glanced at his watch to stop his eyes from making any further descent. It was 9:35 P.M. Frank knew that the girl had lied about Marie-France being associated with the bar. After all, she had lied more than several times in the short time he had been in the bar. But, he had no where else to go. He ordered another red wine. Jasmine had another champagne.

During their conversation, Frank brought up and discussed why he had come to France. He talked about Marie-France, what they had done together, the trip to the flea market, the strange green light coming from the statue, his love for the girl in the photo and her unexplained disappearance. Jasmine seemed interested in this young man who, giving up his teaching career, had remained in her country and who was now searching for a woman with whom he had certainly fallen in love. She was almost sorry for what she had implied earlier about Frank's friend.

Perhaps out of genuine concern, perhaps out of the professional

161

expectations of her boss behind the bar, Jasmine moved closer to Frank, took one of his hands in hers and put it on one of her breasts. Frank tenderly removed his hand and said, *"Desole, Jasmine. Marie-France me manque un peu trop."* Jasmine understood, and in a very unpredictable way, whispered in his ear, "You must leave quietly. My friends at the bar might expect you to take me with you next door. I have never seen the girl in the picture. She has never been here before, and I hope you find her. Good luck my friend."

Thoroughly convinced that everything said earlier about Marie-France ever being in this bar was a lie and that it was just a way of keeping him in her place of work, Frank got up, paid his bill, left Jasmine a substantial *pourboire*, and moved quietly out of the *"Bar Americain"* and into the street. He was happy that he had learned nothing of Marie-France in such a place, and he knew that, sooner or later, he would be successful in finding her. After all, Paris wasn't that big, and Frank knew Paris better than any other city he had ever seen.

Chapter 8

Chaperones

Frank walked out into Rue Blanche and took his place in the flow of the crowd coming from places like the Moulin Rouge and other night spots in the area. The mixture of tourists, streetwalkers, scam artists and restaurant goers moved quickly to their various destinations. Frank entered the first metro station he came to and caught a train headed back to the Latin Quarter. Once there, he grabbed a café noir at one of the little bistros and climbed the steps leading to his top floor apartment.

Frank stopped abruptly in front of his door. His heart jumped. There, tacked to the wooden door, was a note. He took the note off the door and read, "Frank, Please go home. You must not try to find me. I am not for you. We are too different, and you will eventually leave me. I know that. Marie-France" She had seen him at St. Denis! She had heard him call out to her inside the cathedral. And, if she did not love him, he thought, she would never have left a note on his door by taking a chance of running into him as she did so.

The paper Frank held in his hands was enough to kindle the fires of the passion he had for Marie-France for years to come. He would find this girl who, in her note to him, had seemed to question his resolve. He would find her. He would convince Marie-France that she was for him and not for anyone or anything else. But, first, he had to go back to work, and that would start within days. Frank asked himself that evening why Marie-France thought that he was "different" from her. He had loved her, and he had often told her so. She, or so he thought, loved him. Was it money? Frank didn't have much, and Marie-France never gave any indication of coming from a wealthy family. In fact, she rarely mentioned family. She had never put on airs of being a member of the *Tout Paris*, the jet set, and she seemed happy living with him in his little student apartment.

The next morning when he awoke, Frank called his tour company, the CIA, and asked for information about his next student travel group. He learned that his next tour group would be American high school students chaperoned by two female teachers. The group wanted to spend their entire time, ten days, close to Paris. He was asked to work up an itinerary including the Louvre, Napoleon's Tomb, the Eiffel Tower, the impressionist museum at *Jeu de Paume*, Sarcre Coeur at Montmartre, work in a ride on the *bateaux mouches*, visit the Arch of Triumph, Notre Dame Cathedral and then, of his own choice, he was to put in anything else he thought important enough to see. Frank immediately sketched in a visit to St. Denis and the cathedral. Who knows...? He took the rest of the afternoon and worked out time schedules, hotel accommodations and evening meal arrangements. That evening, he had couscous royal at *Le Bon Couscous* near his apartment. Even the owner of the restaurant sat with Frank and discussed the latest developments about his search for Marie-France. After dinner, he went to bed early in preparation for the next day.

Frank met his group the next morning at Charles De Gaulle Airport. Thirty-five high school students, most of them female, two very attractive female chaperones in their late 30's, and three female retirees in their late 60's. Frank made sure everyone had their own luggage (He did not want to return to the airport because someone had forgotten to pick up their bags after getting off the plane.), and he made sure that everyone in the group held up his passport (Too many students had lost their passports in the airport upon disembarking from the plane and going through customs.). After those important checks, he escorted the entire group to the tour bus waiting for them in the parking area of the airport.

Once on the bus, and on the way to the city, Frank gave the Americans an official welcome to France, and he told them about the sights they would see during their stay. He pointed out the huge, white Basilica of Sacre Coeur which jutted up from its promontory in Montmartre, he drew the students' attention to the Seine River, and he challenged them to be among the first in their group to point out the Eiffel Tower.

In spite of the long transatlantic trip they had just taken, most of the students were excited about their first time in the City of Light. A lot of the girls sat up in the bus near Frank, this good looking American guide who would be with them for the next ten days. That he had attracted the attention of these teenagers was evident, and he almost blushed because of it. The chaperones sitting along side him tried out their French on Frank and found themselves a little lacking in comparison to his use of the language.

That observation made the chaperones feel better about the guide who would spend the next week and a half showing them the sights of Paris. Confidence in one's tour guide always makes for a better trip, and all the Americans felt that they were in good hands.

The trip from the airport to the city took about a half hour, and once they had arrived at their hotel in the heart of the Marais quarter, and area under reconstruction and future site of Pompidou Center, Frank helped each student and chaperone get registered, and he made sure they all had a room. Students were placed three and four to a room. The chaperones had rooms to themselves as did the retirees. Once everyone was comfortable and in their own rooms, Frank went to his and freshened up. The group had been given an hour to take showers and get ready for a bus tour of the city.

Frank looked out the window of his room and into the Rue St. Antoine below. At one time in the past, splendid town houses had lined the street. Now, some of these *hotels* were in disrepair, and in front of them, even at this time in the morning, street walkers were already at their posts in doorways or leaning up against the wall of some building. Frank knew that the students would have questions about these heavily mascared and scantily clad young women standing in the street, and he wondered how he would explain this cultural phenomenon. He decided that he would try to focus their attention on the architecture and the restoration taking place. Yeah, right!

Once downstairs, keys were turned in to the reception area, names were called making sure everyone was present, and the group was escorted down a narrow street to an area where the bus was waiting. In this section of the city, the streets were too narrow for the bus to pass in front of the hotel where it would block traffic. The students, chaperones and adult participants on the tour followed Frank who led the group toward the bus. Along the way, some of the students rushed to get close to Frank at the head of the cortege, and one of the girls spoke up and said, "Frank, what are those women doing standing in some of the doorways across the street?" Frank knew from the giggles of the others that the girl already knew the answer to her question, and he added to their insight by saying, "This is Paris, city of high fashion, and those ladies are modeling the latest in lingerie." The whole group roared with laughter, the chaperones smiled, and in a short time, everyone was on the bus and in a good mood for the sightseeing to come.

For a little over one hour, the bus made its way in and out of the narrow streets and larger avenues of the city as Frank, using the P.A. system, gave a verbal history and description of things seen in passing. While moving by the Hotel Ritz, the Arch of Triumph, down the Champs-Elysees, skirting the Louvre, and driving by Napoleon's Tomb, the Eiffel Tower, Sacre Coeur in Montmartre and Notre Dame Cathedral, Frank tried to hold the students' interest by telling stories about each monument which, in a different situation, would have made most historians listen in awe. But, the students were too excited by what they were seeing along the streets to pay good attention. They could not get over the fact that some French people actually carried unwrapped bread, the familiar long baguettes, under their arm as they moved from place to place on their way to and from work or home. They were amused that most of the cars along the streets were smaller than their American counterparts. They noticed that many more French people smoked than did Americans, and they were surprised that almost every other woman they saw had a dog on a leash, dogs which left their feces on the street while their owners seemed not to notice. The students noticed that most of the people in the streets were well dressed, and that every sidewalk café was full with clientele enjoying a coffee, a newspaper and each others' company. These authentic sights, sounds and smells were too much competition for Frank's discourse on monuments, but he didn't mind. The students's distraction also gave Frank the time to scan the streets for the woman he loved. The bus tour was a success. Frank's clandestine search was a failure.

Frank had the bus stop in the Latin Quarter, and the students were told that they could buy their lunch at one of the restaurants in the bustling area full of shoppers, tourists and shopkeepers. Prices were good in the quarter, the food delicious, and just across the river was Notre Dame Cathedral. The group was told to meet in front of the statue of Charlemagne located on one side of the square in front of the cathedral. Once all the students had found a restaurant, the stragglers placed with more outgoing members of the group in order to prevent homesickness from setting in, and the adult participants given last minute instruction on what they would see and do in the afternoon, Frank took the chaperones and other adults to his favorite restaurant, *Le Bon Couscous.*

All the waiters at Frank's favorite restaurant knew him. They greeted Frank with smiles and friendly exchanges in French and colloquial Arabic. Frank and his group were seated in the *caveau* downstairs, and everyone, on Frank's recommendation, ordered couscous royal and Algerian red wine. The food and the wine allowed Frank to learn more about each of the adults in the group. One of the older travelers was very well off financially, and it was she who paid the bill for the entire group.

All of the older women in this new group had known each other for some time, and it was their first time in Paris. The two female chaperones, both in their thirties, were quite attractive. One of them, Diane, was married, and her husband had to stay home and work while his wife did what many foreign language teachers do—spend their vacations showing their students the joys of their target language country. The other chaperone, Allison, was single, very pretty and coquettish. Frank liked her for she flirted not only with him, but with all the waiters, too. One of the waiters came over to Frank and whispered to him, "She is something, huh?" Frank smiled in agreement. Then, the waiter leaned toward him and again whispered, "Your friend, the pretty one, Marie-France, came in last night."

Chapter 9

Lingerie

At first, Frank thought that he had misunderstood the waiter; Algerian French has its idiosyncracies. Everyone at Frank's table was talking at once and they were animatedly happy about their first day in Paris. There were a few others in the restaurant, and they, too, were in conversation, so Frank asked the waiter to repeat what he had just said. When the waiter confirmed that he had seen and spoken to Marie-France, Frank excused himself from the table and took the waiter aside where he asked, "She was alone? Did she say anything about me? When was she here?" The waiter explained that she had stopped in very late, that she seemed to be looking for someone, maybe Frank, and that she was carrying something. "What?", said Frank. "I am not sure.", replied the waiter. "I think it was a statue."

—Did she say where she had been, where she was going?

—Nothing!

—What did she say before leaving?

—Trois fois rien!

Frank returned to his table, and his lunch companions asked if something was wrong. Frank said no. He told them that he and the waiter were just exchanging news, that he often come to this restaurant and that he needed some information about someone they both knew. Allison spoke up by saying, *"Ton grand amour?"* "No, no, just a friend.", lied Frank. He thought it best that he not share any worries he had with his new group. Everyone finished the meal, a few toasts were made with the wine which remained in their second bottle, the bill was paid, and the group left for the meeting place in front of Notre Dame Cathedral.

In spite of Frank's preoccupation with what he had just learned from the waiter at the *Bon Couscous*, he gave his new group a complete tour of the cathedral. He talked about its construction in the 11th and 12th centuries, and he pointed out why some of the statues on the facade of the cathedral were without heads; during the Revolution, the hatred of the Monarchy allowed no distinction when it came to marble or flesh. Thinking that the statues represented kings and queens of France, the revolutionaries had beheaded even the marble statues on the church.

Frank talked about the roof spouts of the cathedral, the gargoyles, which were carved to represent a grotesque human or animal figure and projected out from the stone structure in the form of a rain gutter to carry rainwater away from the limestone walls. Frank made reference to Quasimodo, the bell ringer in Hugo's *Notre Dame de Paris*, and he took the students up the narrow steps leading to the top of the south tower of the cathedral where, one at a time, the students had their pictures taken with their arms around their handsome tour guide. The students invited the chaperones to do the same. Diane, the married chaperone, declined and suggested that Allison and Frank pose together. As they were positioning themselves in front of a gargoyle, Allison leaned in close to Frank and whispered, "Are you involved with someone, Frank?" "I'm not sure.", said Frank. Once they had run out of film, the group headed back down the stone steps, got back aboard the bus and headed back to the hotel.

That evening, after dinner, the entire group went to the Eiffel Tower. Frank made sure that the students took the metro and that they got out at the Trocadero, directly across the river from the tower at exactly 8 P.M. Frank had promised the group a surprise. Making sure that the students followed him, everyone came out of the metro behind the Chaillot Palace. Once outside the train station, Frank walked the students around the building and out onto the terrace, and there it was.

Looming high over the skyline of the left bank of the river, illuminated by thousands of lights which played on surface of the massive steel structure, was the Eiffel Tower. Its magnificence was not lost on the students, and within seconds, the "Awes" and "Wows" were mixed with the sounds of popping flashbulbs. Frank gave the group time to take pictures. Then, at the right moment, he walked the group across the Iena Bridge and up to the tower itself.

Frank took charge of the tickets, and everyone rode elevators to the second and better viewing platform of the tower. Everyone was amazed at the sights seen from the tower. Illuminated by huge spotlights, the students could pick out Notre Dame Cathedral, Sacre Coeur in Montmartre, the Arch of Triumph, and the dome of the Invalides, the huge church and military hospital built by Louis XIV where Napoleon is entombed. The students were able to look down on the well lighted *bateaux mouches,* which from such a height, looked like illuminated caterpillars plying their way up and down the *Seine.*

During all this sightseeing, Allison, the unattached chaperone, moved closer to Frank and slipped her arm around his. She said, "The wind is cold. Do you mind?" Frank looked down at her and said, "Not at all, mademoiselle. What do you think of Paris?" Allison snuggled closer and said, "This is where I want to spend the rest of my life." Some of the female students standing nearby giggled and suggested, "Having fun, Miss Whitesmith?" Shortly, Frank led the entire group back down to the base of the tower. They crossed the bridge, made their way back to the metro and everyone returned late back to the hotel. The night, however, was not over.

Miss Whitesmith, "Allison" to Frank, and her colleague took charge of room checks, and by 11:45 P.M., all the students and the three elderly travelers were in their beds. Frank busied himself in his own room with the itinerary for the next day, and he was just about to finish when a knock came at his door. Frank quickly opened the door thinking that there might be a problem, and there stood Allison. She was wearing a flowing silk charmeuse robe with lacy bell sleeves. She filled out this negligee of a soft shade of lavender in such a way that every inch of the thing she was wearing was straining to keep in check the ample charms it covered. Frank caught himself surveying the garment and contents, then he quickly recovered and said, "Yes, Miss Whitesmith. Is there a problem?"

—I'm not sure, Frank. Would you mind checking one of the rooms with me? I don't want to wake Diane, and something seems to be wrong.

—Sure. What do you think is going on?

—This afternoon, a group of boys from the Italian group which just arrived at the hotel were bothering the girls. The boys were on the steps just outside one of the girls' rooms when we came back tonight.

Frank closed the door to his own room and said, "OK, let's check." Allison slid her arm through Frank's, and the two of them headed down the hallway in the direction of the girls' rooms.

When they came to the suspect room, Frank knocked on the door. Shortly, a sleepy voice came from inside, "Yes. Who is it?" Allison spoke first. "It's Miss Whitesmith. Please open the door." The door opened just a crack, but it was enough to expose the person inside. Frank swallowed hard, for what he saw caused him some concern. A young female student, her body now lighted by the overhead hallway lamp, was wearing only a silk chemise which covered the top of her body. The girl was not wearing panties. Frank carefully kept his eyes locked only on the girl's face, and he asked, "Is everything OK in there?" "Oh, yes." said the girl, "But, a little while ago, some boys were making noise on the stairs. They're gone now. Thank you.", and she closed the door. Frank looked at Allison and said, "I think we had better go in, and I want you to come with me."

Frank knocked again, but this time, his knock was one which carried a message; he was coming in. When the girl came back to the door and opened it, Frank told her, "Please put some clothes on. Miss Whitesmith and I will be coming in."

The girl did as she was told. The tone of Frank's voice let her know that she had no other choice. Frank stepped in and turned on the lights. Two other girls were already in bed, and before Frank could adjust to the light and turn his gaze, the girls pulled up the sheets over their naked bodies. Miss Whitesmith said, "We want to check a few things." Just as she finished her sentence, someone or something knocked over some bottles in the bathroom. Frank asked, "How many girls are there in this room?" "Three.", said Allison. "Then, we have a problem.", said Frank. And, with that, he walked over to the bathroom and opened the door.

There, wearing only their undershorts, bent over each other with their eyes closed like some small animals who, with their sight impeded and therefore thinking that, if they saw nothing, they were then invisible to any prey, were two teenage boys. Frank knew that these boys were not part of the American group, and he asked if they spoke French. Without opening their eyes, they said, "Oui, monsieur."

Without thinking about what he might do if they did not follow his orders, he said in French, "If you move, if you try to do one thing, I will beat you severely. If you understand, nod your heads." The boys nodded affirmatively. Frank stepped back into the bedroom when Allison said, "They are from the Italian group." Frank asked Allison to find the Italian chaperone. She agreed, and as Allison was leaving the room, Frank whispered to her, "Miss Whitesmith, you are beautiful in that gown. Do you have a coverup of some kind. Allison smiled and went to get the Italian chaperone.

Within minutes, Miss Whitesmith, now wearing her bathrobe, returned with a burly, mustachioed man of about fifty years old. He greeted Frank in French, adding that he did not speak English. Frank said that he was sorry that he did not speak Italian, and the two men continued their conversation in French. Frank explained that two boys, still in the bathroom with their eyes closed, were here in the girls' room without the permission of either the American chaperones or the tour guide. The Italian chaperone raised his eyebrows and said, "I will take care of it." Saying that, he walked to the bathroom door, looked in and saw the two boys still locked in position, still blind to their surroundings. The conversation changed to Italian. The boys got dressed, stood at attention in front of their chaperone who slapped both boys hard across the face before Frank could stop him. The chaperone turned to Frank and said, "Is that OK, monsieur?" Frank nodded and the Italian chaperone took the boys out by holding on to one of each of the boys' ears...but, not before taking one last admiring glance at the beautiful American woman dressed in a lavender robe. Allison told Frank that he could leave, and she began to verbally inflict her own punishment on the girls. She told Frank that she would see him in the morning. Frank went back to his room, climbed in bed and fell asleep quickly, and he dreamed of Marie-France. In his dreams, Marie-France was wearing Allison's negligee.

Chapter 10

Jasmine and Lavender

The next morning, when he awoke, Frank was still thinking about Marie-France, sans negligee. At breakfast in the basement of the hotel, Frank sat at Allison's table. The three girls who had attracted the attention of the Italian boys sat next to their chaperone and Frank at the next table. They were teary eyed, and they ate their breakfast in silence. Frank asked Allison if everything was OK, and she responded that some new rules were now in place, and that some apologies had been extended to both chaperones and guide.

Once everyone had finished breakfast, Frank told the group that the day's activities would include a visit to *Les Invalides*, the magnificent 17th century church and military hospital built by the Sun King, Louis XIV. Under the giant dome of the basilica, in a red marble coffin, lies the body of Napoleon Bonaparte. On the bus on their way to Napoleon's Tomb, some of the students asked Frank what the large, seemingly abandoned building was which bordered the banks of the Seine at the quay d'Orsay. Frank told the group that the structure was once a very prestigious hotel and train station that had been designated for demolition. However, a few forward thinking people were talking of making it into an art museum, perhaps one of the most beautiful in Paris.

Soon, the group had arrived at the Esplanade, the spectacular vista 500 yards long which leads up to the domed building housing the tomb. Frank had the group get off the bus and look at the magnificent structure from a distance. Everyone took pictures of their friends with the building in the background.

Once pictures were taken, Frank put the students into some kind of military formation. He wanted them to march up to the structure. After all, in the inner court yard of the massive structure, many French military reviews are held.

Calling cadence, something he had not forgotten from his days as a Marine, Frank marched the students into the area in front of the entrance to the *Invalides.* There, he stopped the group and asked that they listen carefully. Knowing that the happening of the previous evening had dampened the students' enthusiasm; it is a well known fact that, in spite of the guilt of the infraction, students will always side with their own. It is a survival technique, and while the girls were guilty of inviting some boys into their room after curfew, sympathy, in the students mind, was on their side. Maybe that's why Frank proposed that the student group march through the entrance and into the interior of the courtyard of this famous building. After all, *Les Invalides* also served as the National Military Museum of France, and its gates were still guarded by French Army personnel.

Before the students started their march through the gates of the *Invalides,* Frank told them that they would be marching to United States

Marine Corps cadence calls. He informed them that they were to repeat what he uttered and to sing out the words loud and clear with the pride of knowing that they were Americans. Hell, why not? Marines are like that. Those sentiments were not shared with the students, however.

Smiles began to appear on the faces of some of the students. Frank checked for understanding, then, he started them out with the ever familiar, "Forward, march!", and the whole group of about forty students, chaperones and tour participants moved out as one unit across the esplanade leading up to the 17th century monument. Frank then gave them their first call, "I don't want no teenage queen...I just want my M14..., If I die in the combat zone...pack me up and ship me home., Pin my medals upon my chest...tell my momma I did my best., Bury me deep in the sand and clay...When I hit the bottom, you'll hear me say., I wanna be a Drill Instructor...I wanna wear a smokey bear. I wanna be a Drill Instructor...I wanna cut off all my hair., Your Corps!...Our Corps!...My Corps!...Marine Corps!...Houraw!" Every student had boomed out in vocal unison the Marine Corps cadence calls. They had repeated perfectly the words Frank had given them, and before the cadence call had finished, everyone in the group, even the once pouting sirens from the past evening's fiasco at the hotel, was smiling.

The marching and the singing of the group drew the attention of Parisian strollers, the chaperones, and especially Allison, who looked admiringly at Frank, their guide, their leader, their Marine. Even the French military guards threw an admiring glance in the direction of the group's leader. Frank saluted in recognition. The rest of the day was an undisputed success. Allison knew that Frank had cemented the camaraderie of the group perfectly, and she wanted to thank him.

But, that would come later...back at the hotel.

Inside the *Invalides,* the students looked down in awe at the Emperor's tomb. The French had constructed the tomb so that everyone looking on the sarcophagus would have to bow his head. It was said, as Frank pointed out, that Hitler, on his first visit to the tomb during the German occupation, stood in one spot for six hours looking down upon his inspiration. In Frank's mind, that fact was evidence enough to show that the former Nazi was out of his mind, but he left that opinion out of his talk to the students; they were smart enough to figure that out for themselves.

From the tomb of the Emperor, the students moved into the military museum where, for the first time, they saw suits of armor dating from the middle ages, armaments from centuries past, and their biggest attention getting item, Napoleon's stuffed white horse. The three girls who had committed the little indiscretion the night before came up to Frank and apologized for their misbehavior. Frank thanked them for their apology and asked them if they would like to see Josephine's wedding gown. They were delighted. Frank took them to a little area devoted to the first of Napoleon's wives. Allison went along, too, and once again, especially after this rather private tour, the health of the group was intact.

Students were given the rest of the afternoon off as free time. Shopping in Paris was number one on the students' list of things to do, and the chaperones had some gift buying on their minds as well. Frank excused himself from the group, and he told them that he would meet up with them again at dinner that evening. Some free time would give him the opportunity to check his room in the Latin Quarter. Since this new group had arrived, he had not been back to his apartment, and in his heart, he was hoping that somehow, some way, Marie-France would be there waiting for him.

Frank walked back to his apartment along the quay d'Orsay along the *Seine.* It was a beautiful day, and as the river boats passed by, he thought of the night he and Marie-France had walked the same path. He remembered that faint scent of jasmine and lavender which clung to his lover's body. He had held her close as they walked along this same street, and that evening, it had seemed that they were joined at the hips like some Siamese twins. Frank wanted that same closeness. He missed the way her breasts fit his hands

213

and fingers. He longed for the way she breathed when he kissed her neck and bare shoulders, and he wanted to hear the way she uttered his name when they made love. Like waves rushing up on a sandy beach, their love making went over and over in his mind, and before long, he was back in the Latin Quarter.

Frank made his way to the entrance of his building, and he climbed the stairs quickly to the door of his apartment. No note! He unlocked the door and went in. There, on the little kitchen table was the statue, and taped to its body was an envelope. Frank opened it immediately, and inside was a note from Marie-France.

> Frank, Why have you not gone home? Why did you stay? What are you doing? If you love me, you must do two things. First, please get rid of the statue. Second, only if you love me, meet me in two weeks time, September 10, at *Le Bon Couscous*. I will be there with someone I want you to meet. Marie-France

Frank could not contain his happiness. He was going to see Marie-France again, and soon! But, who was this mysterious person Marie-France was going to have him meet? Could

A Hint of Jasmine and Lavender
An Erotic Romance

Marie-France have taken another lover? No, impossible, thought Frank. They had shared too much together. They had been lovers, and they had been happy together. Frank freshened up, changed clothes and made himself ready to meet his tour group for dinner. He went over to the window looking down on the street scene below. There was no sign of Marie-France. Before he left his apartment, he picked up her note again and breathed in the faint scent of jasmine and lavender which still lingered on the paper she had used.

Chapter 11

Temptation

Frank arrived early at the restaurant where Allison's students were to have dinner. Before too long, everyone had arrived, and the entire group was on fire with the excitement generated from the free time they had been given. Laughing, talking about the purchases they had made that afternoon, and happy with the things

217

they had seen earlier that morning made the restaurant come alive with the animated descriptions of everyone's free time excursions. It was as if the students had become part of a giant juke box, and each individual's music selection was playing at once.

Allison was radiant in a new dress purchased in one of the upscale Parisian boutiques. The dress and the decolletage it offered only enhanced the appeal of Allison's well- turned body, and Frank could not help letting his eyes admire the sight. His gaze did not escape the sharp eyes of Diane, Allison's co-chaperone either. Frank, noticing that he had been perhaps too observant, quickly inquired about their afternoon's activities.

Allison said that she had purchased her first Parisian original, the dress that she was wearing, and she asked Frank what he thought of it. Glancing first at Diane, and acknowledging her knowing glance seconds before, Frank said that the dress and its wearer were stunning. In spite of the noise coming from the students, some of them picked up on the adults' conversation, and the noise seemed to increase in proportion to comments attributed to Frank's compliments. Both the dinner and the purchases made during the day were a success.

At the end of the meal, and because of it being the last night in Paris for Allison's group, the students were given an extended curfew until midnight, a generous gesture to make for most teachers in charge of high school students. But, Allison's students had proven themselves to be trustworthy, especially after rules were strictly enforced, and they all knew that no one traveled outside the hotel alone. Chaperones and the other adults in the group were asked what they wanted to do. Some wanted to try the *Folies Bergere* and experience a night of

French cancan. Others wanted to have an after dinner coffee and dessert at the Jules Verne, the restaurant de luxe on the Eiffel Tower. Allison and Diane wanted to go to a discotheque on the Champs-Elysees, and they asked Frank to be their escort. He agreed.

The two chaperones and Frank arrived on the Champs-Elysees a little after 9 P.M. On the same side of the avenue located close to Fouquet's, the trendy bistro/café, and secluded in a dark corner of an adjacent building, was one of the most frequented disco-theques in Paris, *Le Bouquet.* To get in the place, you had to walk up to a green door in the center of which was fitted a small glass window on hinges. You knocked on the door, and the window opened exposing a man's face. The face looked you over, and if you fit the description of those who might prove interesting, you were let in. Frank knocked, the window opened, a face peered outside, and what it saw was a guy with two beautiful women, and one of them was wearing a very provocative dress. They were let in immediately.

Once inside, Frank and his two friends were escorted to a table next to the dance floor. Frank ordered drinks for everyone at his table. Arabs in native headdress, Americans in both formal dress and blue jeans, beautiful women from every European country and rich men from all over the world could be seen whirling about the dance floor and wining and dining their companions at tables lighted only by candles. The music was loud and exciting, and the two American chaperones were delighted with Frank's choice of night spots. Allison innocently suggested that Frank and Diane join the others on the floor for the first dance.

Frank extended his hand toward Diane and said, *"A votre service, Madame."* Diane politely declined and said that she was tired and that she would rather just watch the crowd.

223

Then she added, "You two would draw some looks. You do it." Frank said, "Great! Allison could show off her new dress." That's all that Allison needed, and she got up and motioned for Frank to follow her out on to the floor.

The first song was a mixture of African and Caribbean rhythm, and the lyrics were in French. As she danced to the beat, Allison kept her eyes on Frank, and she knew that he liked what he saw. Her body vibrated in sync with the music perfectly, and every step she took was meant to break Frank's will to resist the temptation of reaching out and grasping what she was displaying. How he managed to resist that temptation was surprising even to Frank. Then, the music slowed, and a love song by Yves Montand was piped out over the sound system. Allison offered her arms to Frank, and he took them. The two dancers did draw some admiring glances. Allison's stunning dress, her grasp of the man with whom she was dancing, and the unintelligible things she seemed to be whispering in his ear captured the attention of more than several women who were or seemed to be envious. Once the song had finished, Frank called their attention to the time. It was getting close to the time they needed to get back to the hotel in time for curfew. So, the three Americans called a halt to a wonderful evening and made their way back to the hotel.

All the students were on time for bed checks, and that was much appreciated by chaperones and guide. Some student groups, knowing that it was their last night in Paris and believing that little could be done if infractions of the rules should occur, would often take advantage of the timing before their departure the next day. So, the head chaperone, Allison, accompanied by Frank, made her rounds going into each room and checked one final time each student. While she did so, Frank listened to the students as they told him about their last days in Paris. For these students, it was the best trip they had ever taken. Frank knew that in no other time in their lives would they ever travel so far with so many of their close friends. Frank had made such trips when in the Marines, but he had to admit that he never had participated in such educational activities nor had he visited such wonderful places as had these students, and he was happy that these students, Allison's group, did not have to serve in the military.

Once all the students had been accounted for and in their rooms, Allison took Frank aside and said,

A Hint of Jasmine and Lavender
An Erotic Romance

"Frank, could you come to my room in fifteen minutes? I have something for you." Frank nodded in agreement and went back to his own room. On some occasions, the chaperones of various groups would give their guide a well-earned tip, the customary *pourboire*, out of sight of everyone else so as to preserve some degree of anonymity. Frank was sure that this was the case.

Fifteen minutes went by quickly. Frank quietly knocked on the door to Allison's room. The door opened slowly, and once Allison had confirmed who was there, she motioned for Frank to come in. The interior of the room was dark, and except for three scented and flickering candles, no other source of light existed. Allison closed the door behind her and stepped between Frank and the burning candles. Silhouetted in the light of the candles, Allison was wearing the same negligee she had on the night before, but this time, she wore nothing underneath. She came closer to Frank, and as she approached, she let her negligee slip off her shoulders and onto the floor.

Frank didn't say a word. He could hardly breathe. Allison took one of his hands in hers, and with Frank's hand, she cupped one of her voluptuous breasts. She manipulated his fingers over her now erect nipple, and she took his other hand in one of hers and, ever so slowly, slid it down across her firm and flat belly and into the wetness between her legs. Then, she said, "Frank, This is my last night in Paris. Everything you just touched is yours if you want it."

To himself, Frank uttered, "Oh, merde!" Then, he took Allison in his arms and held her tightly and sincerely. In her ear, he whispered, "Allison, You are one of the most beautiful women I have ever seen. Had I met you months ago, I would have asked you to take me home with you. I would have followed you. But, I am in love with a woman I met here. She left me weeks ago, and while she doesn't seem to love me, I need to know why she left me. I need to know that before I open my heart to another. Please forgive me." He kissed her softly on both cheeks, turned, and walked out of the room and closed the door to Allison's room behind him.

The next morning, everyone had breakfast quickly. There was electricity in the air. Bags were placed aboard the bus, and the students were awarded last glimpses of the City of Light as the bus made its way to Charles De Gaulle Airport for the trip back to the United States. Frank accompanied the group to the airport. Once there, he made sure all the students had their passports, goodbyes were said and tears were shed. Frank again kissed Allison on both cheeks, *a la francaise,* and he waited until Allison's plane was making its way along the runway for takeoff. He then returned to his apartment in the Latin Quarter.

Chapter 12

Splash!

That afternoon, after he had gotten back into his apartment along the *Seine,* Frank saw to it that the statue left on his table by Marie-France was carefully wrapped in plain brown paper and tied securely with string. He placed the package on his kitchen table knowing that, later in the evening, he would do what he had been instructed to do by Marie-France. He left his apartment and checked into his office at the CIA and told his employers that he would be able to take on only individuals who wanted to do a tour of Paris on a day-by-day basis for the next week. He added that, for the following week, he would not be available at all. One of the secretaries told him that a woman named Allison had called and that she wanted Frank's employers to know what a wonderful job he had done for her and her students. Reports like that were always good. Frank then checked his mail, and he found a letter mailed from the United States.

Splash!

The return address on the envelope read,

DeMarlo Law Offices
Attorneys at Law
Rochester, New York

Frank opened the envelope and read the very official looking paper inside:

Dear Mr. Sarvey:

Enclosed, please find the Estate Check in the sum of $20,000, representing each beneficiary's share under the terms of the Last Will and Testament of Laurence E. Ford.

235

Thank you for your cooperation and consideration. If you have any questions, please do not hesitate to call or write.

Return addresses, telephone numbers and appropriate signatures were added. Frank looked at the check, and he thought back to his uncle, Larry, who had been the only one to attend Frank's graduation from Marine Boot Camp, Parris Island, South Carolina. Frank's uncle had worked for forty years at a Kodak Company plant in Rochester. His savings were divided evenly between the fourteen nieces and nephews still living. Frank had spoken at his uncle's funeral, and he had forgotten or didn't care about any inheritance which might be forthcoming. Frank said a silent prayer for his uncle whom he had loved, and then, he went to his bank and deposited the check in his account. The money might come in handy and allow him more time, if needed, to remain in France.

Frank returned to his garret apartment in the quarter and sat to work on cleaning the entire place. He performed a Marine Corps field day throughout the apartment, and while he did not scrub the floors with a toothbrush, in a few hours, the apartment was spotless. Once that had been done, Frank showered. He let the hot water pound down upon him cleansing everything from him but the thoughts of Marie-France which were running through his mind. He thought about the meeting with her which was to take place in just a little over a week. He thought about the person she wanted him to meet. But, no matter who it might be, Frank loved her, and just seeing her again would clear up for him the yet unanswered questions he had.

Frank did admit to himself that, if this mysterious person Marie-France wanted him to meet was either a fiancé or another lover, or worse, an estranged husband, all his effort, all his patience and all his faithfulness in the face of some very strong temptation would have been in vain. If Marie-France wanted Frank to know that she loved anyone but him, then that would cause a wound almost impossible to heal. Such a thing, Frank told himself, could not be possible. He knew Marie-France better than that.

That evening, Frank had dinner at a little bistro along the *Seine.* He had a few beers, and when it was dark enough, he went back to his apartment, picked up the package lying on the table, and went back out into the Paris night. When he got to the river, he walked directly out onto the *Pont Neuf*, the oldest bridge in Paris. When he had reached the center of the first span of the bridge, Frank stopped and looked over the railing and on to the humourous and grotesque figures carved into the structure's stone work. Comic characters such as Tabarin, the 17th century French farceur, and the Italian, Pantaloon, as well as a host of gapers and pickpockets, their faces forever locked in stone, looked back at Frank and seemed to mock him knowing what he was about to do. In front of these witnesses in stone, he was about to get rid of one of the things which might have caused Marie-France to leave him.

Making sure that no one else was on the bridge, he held the package out over the railing, and with a determined release of his grip on the thing, he let it fall from his hands. He watched as it spiraled down toward the swirling waters. It made a splash, and it went out of sight forever into the dark waters of the *Seine*. Nothing, not even a slight green glow remained of the statue, and Frank knew that, years from that moment on the bridge, the strong, surging waters of the river would roll and toss what remained of the statue out into the mouth of the *Seine* near the

Atlantic Ocean. One chapter in Frank's life had ended, and at the same precise moment, another began.

During the rest of the week, Frank took time to put his papers in order. He wanted to make sure that his teacher certification in the United States was still valid. With the jettison of the stature, getting rid of a slight trace of ridiculous thoughts about one's attachment to the supernatural, one bridge had been burned completely. He checked his bank book, and he found that he was not rich, but his uncle's legacy and the money he had saved before coming to France would allow him to invest in some sort of modest home outside Paris. And, his expenses were minimal while he lived in a third floor apartment in the Latin Quarter. If, in his meeting with Marie-France and this stranger or strangers she wanted him to see meant that he could no longer be close to the one he loved, he would return to the United States and resume his career in teaching.

Frank checked his passport, and he even wrote letters of inquiry concerning teaching positions, and on a whim, he addressed one such inquiry to a place in upstate New York called Saratoga. Why not? He already had a map of the place picked up from one of the *bouqinistes* along the banks of the

Seine. Then, he began to prepare himself mentally for the next week's meeting.

Chapter 13

Battle Plans

In the days to come, and in preparation for his meeting with Marie-France and her mysterious guest, Frank checked his wardrobe. He still had a couple good sports jackets, some good looking trousers, nice dress shirts and a couple ties. The clothes he wore for his job with the tour company only demanded blue jeans, pull overs and sneakers. After all, riding on a bus and visiting museums all day did not demand much in the way of style. For dinner, Frank always wore something a little more appropriate, but for his luncheon with Marie-France, he wanted to wear his best. Would he bring roses? What color? Did red mean passion? Did yellow indicate devotion? He decided that he had better get it right, even if it meant nothing, so he decided to pay a visit to a florist.

The *Marche aux fleurs* was located right on the *Quay aux fleurs* not far from Notre Dame Cathedral and within walking distance from Frank's apartment. It took him minutes to reach the flower stalls and once there, he took his time walking around drinking in all the beautiful colors and bathing himself in the aroma of all the delightful smells rising up from the baskets brimming over with flowers from all parts of France. Every flower imaginable could be purchased here. Finally, he found a stall which specialized only in roses, and working there was a very handsome woman who appeared to be in her 40's. Frank walked up to her and said, *"Excusez-moi, Madame, mais, j'ai un petit probleme. Pouvez-vous m'aider?"*

Frank had learned since coming to France that people in that country do not like to be disturbed while they are at work. However, if asked to help, especially when someone seems to need their advice, the French will bend over backwards and go to extremes in their attempt to be of service. The flower seller was no exception to this rule. She smiled at this handsome young man in need and said, *"Mais, bien sur, monsieur. A votre service."*

Frank explained to the woman that he was going to purchase some flowers for a lady within the next few days, and that he was unsure about roses, their color and what each color might mean. The woman's eyes lit up. She recognized in Frank a serious young man in need of her expertise. She began her explanation by saying that color, especially in roses, was important. She added that, if the woman in question was the man's lover, then the color red should be considered. The woman looked into Frank's eyes as if searching for some kind of affirmation. Smiling, she further explained that cardinal red meant sublime desire, fiery red indicated flames of passion. When she saw Frank blush, she knew that her lesson was holding her listener's attention.

The woman continued, and she never took her eyes off Frank as if to read his reaction to her words. She went on to explain that the color yellow sometimes meant jealousy. A surprised look came across Frank's face because he immediately thought of the song, "The Yellow Rose of Texas...", and he wondered why someone would sing such words about a woman who must have been true to her love. The rose seller went on to say that the white rose indicated loyalty as well as penetrating and platonic love. Frank decided that there was nothing platonic about his love for Marie-France. Pink, Frank was told, meant, "I am proud of you." Then the woman said, "What kind of a rose is this girl?"

Frank smiled and said, "Almost all the above." He thanked the well-informed rose seller for her help, and he said that he hoped to see her again soon. She smiled in recognition and went about her work. On his way out of the flower stall, Frank noticed that some of the stalls carried jasmine and lavender in well-arranged displays. He thought that a scattering of a few sprigs of the two flowers might add a touch of something to a bouquet of roses.

On his way back to his apartment, Frank stopped by *Le Bon Couscous* and inquired whether Marie-France had come in during the past few days. The owner/manager said that she had not been in lately, and he inquired whether Frank wanted to leave a message. Frank shook his head and said that he would be in for lunch on September 10, just a few days from now, and that he would see her then. At that point, the restaurateur said something which stopped Frank in his tracks. "Yes, someone has reserved the entire *caveau,* the entire basement area of the restaurant, on behalf of Marie-France. A man called earlier this morning."

Frank asked if the man had left his name. "Yes, a certain Monsieur Geoffroy Gagnon." Marie-France's family name! Was she married? Frank asked his friend if there was anything else.   The restaurant owner told him that Monsieur Gagnon had sent his business card. Frank asked if he could see it. The owner went to his office and returned immediately with the card. It read:

Geoffroy Gagnon, Oenologue

Chef de Cave, Moet & Chandon

Specialiste a Dom Perignon

What would a wine maker, head of vintage, be doing making a reservation for Marie-France? Frank returned the business card to his friend, the restaurant owner and left with the name, Dom Perignon, running through his mind.

253

Frank spent the rest of the day walking through the Latin Quarter in contemplation of what he had just been told. He took the bustling Boulevard St. Michel, the "Boul Mich," where students still shopped for books, records and writing material. He peered into the publishing houses, bookshops and café terraces hoping to catch sight of the woman he loved. Having no luck picking out Marie-France in the crowds of people going about their business, he continued down the Rue Mouffetard past umbrella shops, *tabacs*, and bistros, and he found himself in the old Roman arena, the outlines of which were still preserved and protected for all to see. He sat down on one of the ancient stone benches 2nd century Romans must have used when viewing the gladiator fights which took place there. In a few days, not far from this historic place, Frank would have his own face-to-face encounter, and he was determined to come out the victor. He wanted to win once again the heart of Marie-France.

Chapter 14

Countdown

During the next few days, Frank busied himself with reading, strolling through some of the areas he had never visited before, and preparing for his meeting with Marie-France. That meeting, a mysterious luncheon with his former lover and perhaps a certain Monsieur Gagnon, would take place tomorrow, and he wanted to be ready.

The name on the business card! Now, he remembered! He had seen that name before. That day he had spent on the Champs-Elysees sipping tea and watching people go by, he had seen the same name on the marquee hanging outside the Dom Perignon Headquarters on the largest avenue in Paris. That's where he had seen the name! "Geoffroy Gagnon." Who was he? Frank was soon going to find the answers to all his questions.

Frank thought about the flowers, their colors and what Marie-France might think if he brought them to her. He set off for the flower market, and he wanted to get there before the stalls closed for the day. He went back to the woman who had given him so much information, and she smiled broadly as he approached her. He asked that she pick out one, outstanding, fiery red rose. As she was doing so, he asked the woman what she thought about making a bouquet by surrounding the rose with sprigs of jasmine and lavender. She told Frank that the juxtaposition of the rose among the fragrant white petals of the lavender would offer a certain sensuality to the gesture. She added that it would be like a well-dressed lady wearing a seductive perfume. Frank liked her analogy knowing all too well that the rose represented Marie-France. The perfume, he hoped, would come later. The flower vendor made a special bouquet of the rose, the spikes of lilac-purple lavender and sprigs of white jasmine. She wrapped the whole in soft white tissue paper and handed it to Frank saying, *"Bonne chance, Monsieur. Elle doit etre tres speciale, cette femme."* Frank nodded his head in agreement, and he paid his bill giving the woman a substantial tip for her efforts.

That evening, Frank went out again and walked along the quays of the *Seine.* He stopped in the middle of the Pont St. Michel and looked down at the *bateaux mouches* plying the waters below. The brightly lit boats were filled to capacity with merrymaking tourists, some having dinner and sitting at candle-lighted tables while listening to the audio programs describing the monuments illuminated by artistically located spots along the banks of the river. Frank could make out the monologues of French, German, Japanese and Spanish coming up from the boats as they passed by.

Some of the tourists on these boats looked up at Frank and waved. He smiled and waved back, and he tried to give the impression that he was having as much fun as they were aboard those wonderful sleek craft. Paris, he thought, is beautiful any time of the day or night. How much more that beauty would be enhanced if Marie-France were with him on this bridge, her arm in his breathing in the same sights, the same air. He could wave back at these animated tourists in their boats and say to himself, "You see, I have my own Venus de Milo with me tonight."

Frank continued on across the bridge and on to the *Ile de la Cite*, the largest of the two main islands located in the middle of the river. He walked on to the *Conciergerie*, the infamous prison which dates from the 14th century and which held such incarcerated souls as

Ravaillac, the assassin of Henri IV; Charlotte Corday, the assassin of Marat; the chemist, Lavoisier; Robespierre and 2,660 others who, along with Marie-Antoinette, met their death under the guillotine. Frank decided that this type of place was not where he wanted to be, and he turned around and headed back toward the left bank of the *Seine.*

Frank decided to take the Pont Solferino, one of the few pedestrian bridges which crossed the river. There, stationed like sentinels at prescribed intervals along the bridge, were young lovers locked in statue-like embraces. Some of these human sculptures reminded Frank of Rodin's statues he had seen weeks ago, and he imagined that, if he had the talents of the creator of "The Kiss," he could find his models here on the Solferino Bridge. As he walked by these flesh and blood love scenes, Frank tried to keep his eyes focused on the walkway or the river, but, as surreptitiously as was possible, he scanned the faces of each female he encountered. He was still searching for one face all the while hoping that it was not among those he passed. His hopes were fruitful, and he reached the other side of the river and headed back to the Latin Quarter.

Frank climbed the stairs to his floor and came to the door of his apartment. There, tacked on the door, was another note. He took the note off the door and opened it. It read, "Frank, Tomorrow, please be kind. Do not be angry with me. I want you to meet someone very dear to me, and you must be understanding. If you ever loved me, you will do as I say and not be angry with me or with the man I want you to meet. M-F"

So, there it was. There was another man. Her husband? Why would Marie-France want Frank to meet him? Why now? What would come of it? What would he do with the little bouquet which now seemed incongruous among everything now taking place. Blue jeans or more formal dress? What did it matter if it was Brooks Brothers or Wrangler? At that point, Frank concluded that he had nothing to lose. He knew what he was going to do, what he was going to wear and what he was going to say at this luncheon. He even knew how long he was going to remain in Paris, and for some reason, the tune and lyrics to "When Johnny comes marching home..." began running through his mind like some melody picked up by some schoolboy who was in need of distraction. Frank kept that tune in his mind as he showered, laid out his best clothing, made sure his flowers were still fresh in the fridge, and went to bed.

He did not dream.

Chapter 15

Champagne Send Off

The next morning, Frank opened his eyes with a fresh and positive feeling about himself. He felt the best he had felt in weeks, and he wanted to meet the day head on. By 6 A.M., he had taken coffee at one of the *brasseries* in the quarter. He read a copy of <u>Le Monde</u>, and he breathed in the sounds, sights and smells of an early morning Paris. Frank had gotten used to the sounds of the 4 cylinder engines, the passenger buses, the diesel trucks and the hustle and bustle of people going to and from work. He liked those sounds, they were foreign and contrasted sharply with his memory of things back in his small home town in Pennsylvania. As he drank his coffee, he knew somehow that today would be an important day in his life. Whether he would continue to savor the sounds of Paris or learn to love again in the stillness of small town life depended on what might take place a few hours from now in a little restaurant not far from where he was drinking his café noir.

Frank had planned to arrive at the restaurant around noon. He did not want to be early; that might look too desperate. He made a call to Air France and got the latest updates on one-way fares to the United States, picked a price and made reservations with a fourteen-day advance. He was told that he could cancel those reservations with no penalty if he so chose. Frank doubted that any cancellation would take place, and that made him sad. He went down to his favorite used book shop, "Shakespeare Publications", located close to the river and just a few streets away from his apartment building. There, he purchased a copy of love poems by Ronsard, and read over one of his favorites, *Mignonne*.

The poem spoke of the poet's pleading with his love and inspiration to allow him the pleasures of her charms before life and time erased them completely. The poem made him think of what might have been with Marie-France. She had given of herself, but Frank wanted more. Then, Frank went back to his apartment and began preparing for his luncheon with his own muse.

Frank shaved, and as he did so, he composed what he was going to say to Marie-France. He took a shower, and he let the hot water pound down upon him thinking that the soap and hot liquid would wash away any fears he had concerning what his love might say to him. If it was rejection he was about to face, he would want to know why. If it was an effort to explain her sudden disappearance, he would listen. But, the third party in this meeting was disturbing. Who was the "man" in her note? Frank was minutes away from finding the answers to all his questions.

He put on his best dress outfit and looked at himself in the little mirror hanging in his bathroom. He had seen more handsome men, but none more determined. He took his bouquet from the fridge, confirmed that it was still fresh and decided, if nothing else, the flowers were beautiful and they smelled good. He checked his French currency, made sure he had forgotten nothing and left the apartment.

Le Bon Couscous was just a short distance away, and he took his time getting there. Slightly before noon, he walked in the front door of the restaurant. His friend, the manager/owner, winked at him with a big smile, jabbed his finger in a downward motion in the direction of the *caveau*, the basement seating area of the restaurant. Frank knew that Marie-France and her guest had already arrived.

Frank made his way carefully down the winding, stone steps to the *caveau*. Seated in one of the far corners of the eating place, looking more radiant than he had ever seen her before, was Marie-France. She was beautifully attired in a red and white polka dot silk dress that looked like it had been purchased on the Rue Royale, and if it did not come from Villeroy & Boch, he would be surprised. Seated beside Marie-France was a well-dressed man in his early 50's. Both Marie-France and her companion smiled at Frank. The man got up, extended his hand to Frank and said, *"Je suis le pere de Marie-France, Geffroy Gagnon. Elle*

273

me parle beaucoup de vous, Monsieur."
Marie-France's father! Now what?

Frank shook the father's hand, extended the polite verbal greeting, and instead of kissing Marie-France on both cheeks as was accustomed, Frank took her hand in his and said, "I have missed you...very much." She responded, "And, I, you." Frank offered his bouquet to Marie-France, but before she could take it, the manager of the restaurant interceded with a vase already filled with water. He said, *"Permettez-moi!"*, and he carefully arranged the flowers and then placed them appropriately on the table. Marie-France's father said, "Please sit beside my daughter. She has missed you, and she has something to tell you." Frank did as he suggested.

Marie-France took Frank's hand in hers, looked him straight in the eyes and said, "Frank, I was afraid that you were going home at the end of the summer, that I would never see you again, and that you were thinking that I did not love you...and that stupid statue..."

—"It's gone.", said Frank.

—"Why did you stay?"

—"It was impossible to leave you."

—"And, your job back in the United States?"

—"Not important."

—"Then, will you stay here?"

275

—"Only if you wish."

—"I do wish. And, now, I must tell you why."

—"Yes?"

—"I love you, Frank."

At that point, Monsieur Gagnon interjected, "Monsieur, what do you think of my daughter?" Without any hesitation, and while looking into the eyes of the woman for whom he had searched for weeks, Frank said, "Monsieur Gagnon, I want to share the rest of my life with your daughter. I want to breathe the same air, hear the same sounds, taste the same foods, smell the same scents and feel and experience the same emotions as she does. And, if she allows it, and with your blessing, I want to wake every morning with her in my arms, and, as she opens her eyes, I want to whisper in her ear, 'You are my reason for being, and I will always love you.' Of all the women I have ever met, your daughter, Monsieur, is the one who has inspired me to do what I never thought I would do; I left a promising career, I have remained in a country not of my origin, and I have lost my heart to a woman I love more than life itself. And, Monsieur, if I had to do it all over again, I would not change a second in all the hours I have spent in your country. If your daughter were to tell me to leave and never come back to Paris, I would obey. But, my heart, Monsieur, would never be the same. It would be broken, but I would continue to live, and the memory of your daughter would forever be on my mind."

"Bravo!" shouted the *maitre d'* who, standing near by and next to the manager of the *Bon Couscous* listening while waiting for the three people to order, betrayed his presence. Realizing that he might have been overly expressive in his approval of Frank's answer to the older man, the two restaurateurs moved back away from the table. Monsieur Gagnon looked at his daughter who, tears streaming from her eyes, kissed Frank for the first time in weeks fully on the mouth.

"Monsieur Sarvey," said the father, "I would like you to come to my office on the Champs-Elysees tomorrow. My company, Dom Perignon, Do you know it?, is in need of an American representative." And, he handed Frank his business card. Frank said that he would love to stop by the office, and that he knew exactly where it was. "And the time?" inquired Frank. "I will expect you around 9 A.M. Now, I will leave you two. I have many things to do today." He kissed his daughter, shook hands with Frank, made arrangements with the restaurant manager for the bill

279

giving him his business card, and walked up and out of the restaurant.

The two young lovers kissed again. They had a quick lunch and made plans to go to Frank's apartment in the Latin Quarter. Frank told Marie-France that he had a surprise for her. "Have you ever heard the story about a man who gives his lover perfume?" Marie-France said, "No. What is it about?" Frank answered that is was about the rest of their lives. Nothing could interrupt the two lovers' conversation, not even the manager of the *Bon Couscous* who brought a bottle of Dom Perignon to the table and placed it next to a bright red rose, and as if embalmed by its fragrance enhanced by a hint of jasmine and lavender, the two lovers discussed plans on which to build the rest of their life.

Allen R. Remaley

Saratoga Springs, New York

Scottsdale, Arizona

November 2003

About the Author

Allen R. Remaley is a veteran of thirty-six years of teaching at the secondary level of education. After his honorable discharge from the United States Marine Corps, he completed his masters degree in French at Penn State University and earned a doctorate at the State University of New York at Stony Brook. Named the "Outstanding Secondary Teacher of Foreign

Languages in the State of New York in 1984," Dr. Remaley is presently employed at Union University in Schenectady, New York where he teaches in the Graduate School of Education. He makes his home in Saratoga Springs, New York and in Scottsdale, Arizona.

CPSIA information can be obtained at www.ICGtesting.com
Printed in the USA
LVOW132346100912

298263LV00001B/7/A